THE POISON GANG

Young entrepreneur and inventor Dick Turner is framed for a crime he didn't commit by unscrupulous business rivals Morris and Ayres, who then blackmail him for his inventions. But Morris disappears, after publicly quarrelling with Turner. Then Ayres is murdered and Turner becomes chief suspect for the police investigation. However, when Turner's fiancée calls in the help of John Blackmore, the famous investigator, he soon discovers there's an even greater and sinister criminal conspiracy at work . . .

Books by Derwent Steele
in the Linford Mystery Library:

THE AVENGERS
THE PHANTOM SLAYER

DERWENT STEELE

THE POISON GANG

Complete and Unabridged

LINFORD
Leicester

First published in Great Britain

First Linford Edition
published 2011

British Library CIP Data

Steele, Derwent.
 The poison gang. - -
 (Linford mystery library)
 1. Inventors- -Fiction. 2. Extortion- -Fiction.
 3. Businessmen- -Crimes against- -Fiction.
 4. Private investigators- -Fiction. 5. Detective
 and mystery stories. 6. Large type books.
 I. Title II. Series
 823.9′12–dc22

 ISBN 978–1–4448–0801–8

Published by
F. A. Thorpe (Publishing)
Anstey, Leicestershire

Set by Words & Graphics Ltd.
Anstey, Leicestershire
Printed and bound in Great Britain by
T. J. International Ltd., Padstow, Cornwall

This book is printed on acid-free paper

1

Harry Cartwright Interferes

'You can cry your eyes out, my girl, but it will make no difference to me. Unless you do what I ask I'm going to charge Dick Turner with the murder of Morris and with stealing the five thousand pounds he carried.'

'But he's innocent, you know that, Mr. Ayres,' a girl's voice pleaded. 'You swore you would ruin him, and I suppose any beastly way is good enough for you.'

The voices dropped to a whisper. Harry Cartwright, an eavesdropper by accident, wished that he could slip away without these people seeing him. As that was impossible he could only stand quiet until they left the room.

Called north to give evidence in a forgery case, the Spring weather had tempted John Blackmore to make the journey by road. The return had hardly begun when a downpour of rain drove them to shelter in Dipton, one of the busy little Lancashire towns that surround Manchester by the dozen.

Whilst Blackmore was phoning Mechlinburg Square to find if anything urgent had turned up in his absence, Cartright had wandered into the quiet reading room of the Dipton Hotel. In a screened recess he came across a chess-board on which a game had been played to an interesting finish. Studying the problem of the mated king, he suddenly realised that two other people had entered the room, and that he was listening to a very private conversation.

'You're a rich man, why can't you leave Dick alone?' the girl's voice flared out. 'He's paid for the mistake he made — ten times over. Since you sacked him he's worked day and night to make good — why can't you give him a chance, Mr. Ayres?'

'Because business is business, my dear, and because I won't be defied by a whipper-snapper who ought to be in prison,' answered the man coldly. 'I've asked him to sell that invention of his, and I've made him a generous offer.'

'He'll never sell it, least of all to you,' the girl said bitterly.

'Then he'll see the inside of a prison before the night's out!' Ayres exclaimed angrily. 'The signed confession he gave Morris proves him a scoundrel, and this latest business — well, it means a life sentence or the rope.'

'I'm not so sure of that,' replied the girl defiantly. 'One thing, you'll never use that confession because I've — Oh!'

The words ended in a startled little cry as the girl realised the blunder she had made. Peeping round the screen Cartright saw the man smile cynically. He was an elderly man, well dressed and so power-fully built that the secretary began to think that it was well he was hidden there.

'Ah!' said the man. 'I searched Morris' papers yesterday and couldn't find the paper,' said Ayres slowly. 'So you have it, Miss Reed.' He made a sudden grab and snatched at the girl's handbag, which was lying on the edge of the table.

Opening it he pulled out a bundle of

letters, and before the girl could do anything ran through them until he came across a piece of paper, folded in two.

He was unfolding it when a hand reached over his shoulder and pulled it from him. Turning round quickly he saw the smiling face of Harry Cartwright.

'That's no way to recover stolen property,' Harry grinned, 'I don't quite get the argument, but stealing from a lady's bag is bad form.'

Mr. Ayres looked as though he was going to have a fit.

'Who — What? What right have you to butt into a private interview?'

He turned to the white faced girl.

'This is yours, I think, Miss,' he said, and handed her the paper which he had so neatly taken from the old man.

Ayres' face turned a deep crimson, and his arm was raised as if he meant to attack the young man. But he remembered in time that they were in a public hotel, and in spite of the smiling face, something warned him that he would be a different proposition to a terrified girl.

'You think you've been very clever,

young man,' he said briefly. 'But you've done this lady no good by your interference. As for you, Miss Reed — unless you return that paper to me within an hour, then I shall have Richard Turner arrested.'

He got up to leave the table and at that moment John Blackmore appeared in the doorway. Seeing his secretary there he made for his table, as he thought. When he was but three paces away the scowling, purple-faced Ayres elbowed past him and went out of the room, banging the door with a force that nearly shook the tiny reading room.

'Pleasant old party, isn't he, Mr. Blackmore,' said Harry. 'He was robbing this lady so I joined in that argument. Miss Reed,' he said turning to the girl, 'this is my guv'nor, Mr. Blackmore. By the way, you'd better be careful if you did pinch that paper from the old man.'

He gave the warning jokingly, but watched the girl with keen eyes. He could see that she was worried with some trouble, and he hoped that the mention of the famous detective's name would encourage her to confide in them. He little knew that by doing so he was to let John Blackmore into one of the most baffling and fantastic cases that ever came his way, and himself into more scrapes than he had bargained for.

The girl stared at the detective for a few seconds.

'You really are John Blackmore?' she asked, and then, to the astonishment of Blackmore and his secretary, tears began to run down her face.

'But what is wrong, Miss Reed?' asked the detective. 'Is there anything I can do to help you?'

He glanced across at Cartwright, who nodded meaningly, and because he had great faith in his secretary's judgment, he listened while the young man told of what had happened in the room, ending with Jacob Ayres' threat.

'And this paper — this confession?' asked Blackmore at last. 'Did you — er — borrow it from Mr. Ayres?'

The girl looked up from the table where she was sitting listlessly.

'I didn't borrow it — I stole it,' she

answered. 'Dick was tricked into signing it, and it's been held as a threat over his head ever since. Please read it, Mr. Blackmore, and then I'll tell you the kind of man Jacob Ayres is.'

As John Blackmore glanced at the typewritten lines his eyes narrowed.

'I admit that I stole fifty pounds from Henry Morris,' he read aloud. 'As an acknowledgement of Mr. Morris' kindness in forgiving me, I agree to hand over to him all rights in the new two-colour process I have discovered. — Richard Turner.'

John Blackmore's face seldom betrayed his thoughts, but Cartwright was quick to catch the coldness of his tone when he handed the document back to the girl.

'A straightforward confession, Miss Reed,' he said. 'I can easily believe that Mr. Morris lost nothing by overlooking Turner's fault, but Turner must have known what he was signing.'

'He knew, but he was tricked into a position in which he had no choice,' Mary Reed explained. 'Two days before he signed that paper he had asked Mr. Ayres' advice about selling a colour printing process he'd discovered.'

'Had he patented that process?' asked the detective.

Miss Reed shook her head.

'No,' she admitted. 'He was very innocent about those things. Mr. Ayres promised that he would speak to a Rochdale firm about it, and Dick was content to wait. A week later he had to go to the manager's private office. Mr. Morris was out and the office empty. Dick said he couldn't understand it, as Mr. Morris had just sent for him. He was leaving the room when he saw a banknote lying on the floor. He picked it up, and was hesitating whether to place it on the table or keep it until he saw Morris when the manager walked into the room with Mr. Ayres. Before Dick could speak Morris snatched the note out of his hand, and at once accused him of taking it from the safe!'

'Sounds like a frame-up,' murmured Cartwright.

'That's what Dick called it,' said Miss Reed. 'But Morris stuck to this tale, and

Ayres believed him. Dick's mother was very ill at the time, the disgrace of his arrest would have killed her, so Dick gave way and signed this wretched paper. He thought it meant only giving up the profit from one little idea, but Morris has held it over his head ever since, and used it to suck his brains dry.'

'He has invented other things, then?' asked Blackmore.

'Several minor ones,' said Mary Reed. 'He is known as live man in textile chemistry. Well, six months ago his mother died, and soon afterwards he told Morris to do his worst. He was sacked, but with the little money he had he took over a small weaving shed.

'He'd kept the biggest thing of all up his sleeve. It's an artificial silk process that is going to do big things one day. It was not long before Morris found out about it, and since then he has been after it. He has threatened and quarrelled with Dick until everyone in Dipton knows they are bitter enemies.

'A week ago there was a quarrel in the club, and it developed into a fight. Dick gave him a good hiding. Three nights ago Morris disappeared.'

'But beyond their quarrelling, why should Turner fear any charge that Ayres can bring against him?' asked Blackmore. 'Of course, if Ayres has any proof — '

'He says he has,' broke in the girl. 'And he is a very powerful man in Dipton. I am a typist in his works office, and he sent for me this afternoon. He told me that three nights ago he sent Henry Morris to Dick with an offer to buy his patent, and five thousand pounds in notes to pay for it.'

'Can he prove that?' asked the detective.

'He said he can,' sighed Miss Reed. 'He says that he drew the money from the County Bank that afternoon, and that he mentioned to the manager it was the purchase price of Dick Turner's business.'

'That's not so good,' said Harry.

'It's horrible,' said the girl, 'for Dick is known to be desperately hard up,' the girl answered. 'The bank refused him an overdraft, and advised him to sell out to one of the big syndicates.'

'H'm!' murmured Blackmore. 'That certainly gives Ayres a motive for suspecting Turner. And by taking that confession from Morris' desk, I'm afraid you've made things look a hundred times worse.'

'But I had every right to take it,' said the girl indignantly. 'They only got it by a trick.'

'But how will it look when Ayres says that this document was stolen from Morris' desk since he disappeared?' Blackmore demanded. 'Don't you think the police will think it is an attempt to cover up the motive for the crime — for at present there is only Ayres' word that Morris ever went near Turner's place that night.'

There was a moment's silence as the girl took in the meaning of John Blackmore's reasoning. Then she nodded miserably, and asked in a whisper how she could repair the damage she had done.

'By telling Dick Turner what you have told us to-night, and by handing that paper back to Ayres,' said Blackmore

11

briskly. 'You'd better get the car out again, Cartwright, then we'll hear what Turner has to say about this supposed offer of five thousand pounds for his business.'

2

Richard Turner's Position

The detective's powerful car carried them
across Dipton in less than five minutes.
The rain was still falling, and the factory
sites looked drab and unlovely when Mary
Reed pointed to a single-storey shed, almost
hidden by a huge, red brick building.

'That big place is Ayres',' she explained.
'He is terribly rich, and a hard boss, also
he employs about three thousand men.
And this' — she pointed to the small shed
— 'is Dick's workshed. He only employs
forty men, but has the reputation of being
a good man to work for.'

Richard Turner did not open the door
to them, instead they were faced by an
elderly man, whom Mary Reed introduced as, Bill Dale, the foreman.

'You've just missed him,' Dale said,
looking very worried. 'I don't know what
the game is, but not so long since that

13

theer Inspector Moore came in and began firing off questions about old Morris, from the big mill.'

'What did Dick — Mr. Turner say, Bill?' asked Mary anxiously.

'He told Moore to clear out,' said the foreman. 'Said he didn't know anything about Morris, and wasn't wasting his time tryin' to find out.'

'Was Inspector Moore content with that?' asked Blackmore.

'Not him, the big flattie,' Dale growled. 'He brought out a pocket-book, had a squint at it, then he says as information's been laid that Mr. Henry Morris is reported missing, and it was suspected that he'd come to some harm.'

'Did you hear Mr. Turner's reply?' asked Mary Reed.

'Ah, I did,' and Bill Dale grinned. 'Dick said it was a wonder Morris hadn't come to harm afore this, that it's nowt to do with him, anyway, and that he'd be obliged if Moore would go. The old bobby warned Dick to be careful, like, glared at his notes again, and says as Morris was seen walking to this 'ere office at eight-fifteen on Tuesday last.'

'Oh, did Dick admit that?' Mary whispered.

'Like a shot he did,' said Bill Dale, 'and he said that he went out a darned sight quicker than he came in. Then Moore told him that he'd better come along and see Mr. Ayres as things were looking nasty — and he ups and whispers something I couldn't catch. He must have had something important up his sleeve, for the boss turns like a shot and says if that's the game he'll go, as he's been wanting a word with Ayres this while past.'

'How long is it since they left here?' asked Blackmore quickly.

'About ten minutes,' answered the foreman.

'How far is it to Mr. Ayres' house, Miss Reed,' the detective demanded.

'About a mile away, on the Manchester road,' Mary Reed replied. 'Ayres threatened this at the hotel, he hasn't been long. I'm afraid I've put Dick in a terrible position.'

'Don't worry about that,' said Blackmore. 'Ayres has kept his mouth shut for three days, and I don't think he'll be pleased that Moore has butted in now.'

They went back to the car, and Cartwright helped the girl in, and Blackmore turned again to the foreman.

'Will you wait here until Mr. Turner returns, or until you hear from us?' he asked.

'I will that,' growled Dale. 'And if that Moore's making harm to the lad — ' But the rest of the foreman's threat was lost as the car shot away from the kerb and made for the open country.

'Keep a look-out for them,' said Blackmore to his secretary. 'We don't want to pass them on the way. I'm afraid Turner is in a rotten position.' He spoke softly so that Mary Reed should not hear.

They saw no trace of the pair until they were actually in the grounds of Ayres' house and speeding up the long drive.

'There they are,' said Cartwright, 'standing on the steps.'

It was easy enough to tell which was which, for they turned as the car dashed up the drive, and stared in amazement when the occupants got out. Dick Turner stepped forward as he saw the girl, and Blackmore decided that he liked the look of him — a young man of about thirty, with the clean cut lines of an athlete, and a firm mouth that marked the fighter. Inspector Moore was a heavily built man, well over fifty, and with the dour air of a man who gets an idea and sticks to it.

'Inspector Moore?' Blackmore asked — then went straight to the point before the other could answer. 'Miss Mary Reed wishes to speak to Mr. Ayres about his missing manager — if you will allow her two minutes before you see him.'

'Certainly not, sir!' snorted Inspector Moore. 'The whereabouts of Mr. Morris is now a police affair. If Miss Reed knows anything of him it's her duty to tell me.' The front door opened at that moment and a maid stood waiting, looking very surprised at the crowd on the step. 'You'd better all come in with me,' continued Moore. 'We'll ask Mr. Ayres to see us together.'

Behind the Inspector's back Harry Cartwright grinned, for he knew that was just what his employer wanted. He'd worked it very neatly.

They found Mr. Ayres finishing dinner, and entertaining one guest — a fellow in evening dress, who sported a monocle, and whom, Mary Reed whispered to Blackmore, was Dr. Hibbet, Dipton's fashionable physician.

'Sorry to bother you at this time of night, sir,' began Inspector Moore. 'But we've had a complaint that Henry Morris, your manager, is missing. His housekeeper says he hasn't been home since last Tuesday, and that she's sure something has happened to him.'

'Was it necessary to interrupt my dinner to tell me this, and why have you brought this crowd along?' asked Ayres, staring at Blackmore and his secretary.

'I asked Turner because I'm told that Morris visited his shed at eight-fifteen on Tuesday night, and I've a few questions to ask him in front of you, sir,' Moore explained. 'Miss Reed knows something about Morris, I believe — the others I met on your doorstep with her.'

'My name is Blackmore — John Blackmore — and this is my secretary,' the detective said quietly. 'We have been asked by Miss Reed to help her find the missing man — I understand that is also Turner's wish.'

As John Blackmore mentioned his name Jacob Ayres started. In the recent case of forgery which had brought the detective and his secretary to the Midlands, the local papers had given prominence to his name, and the sight of him in his dining-room unsettled Ayres for the moment. Then, with a little shrug, he smiled, and began to toy with a liqueur glass that stood on the table in front of him.

'What do you want to know, Moore?' he asked, his hand still on the glass.

'First of all, is Morris really missing, or have you sent him away on business?' demanded Moore bluntly.

'I sent him to see Dick Turner. I have not set eyes on him since eight o'clock on Tuesday,' Ayres answered slowly.

'You've no reason to think he would leave Dipton on his own?' the Inspector asked.

There was a long pause before the

mill-owner replied. Then, smiling, he leaned back in his chair and looked straight at the Inspector.

'I have no reason to think that Mr. Morris would leave the town without notifying me,' he replied.

'Five thousand pounds is a temptation, even to a man in Morris' position,' suggested John Blackmore. 'We know that he carried that sum, and if others knew it — '

'I've trusted Henry Morris for thirty years,' interrupted Jacob Ayres coldly. 'I've no reason to doubt him now.' He looked at the Inspector. 'I think you said you had questions to ask Turner, Inspector, not me?'

'That's right, sir, and I hope other people will remember it,' he said shooting an angry glance at Blackmore. 'Now, Turner, it's no secret that you had many a quarrel with Mr. Morris, and that you knocked him down in the club last week.'

'It's no secret, and he deserved more than I gave him,' answered Richard Turner quickly. 'We needn't beat about the bush. I've no time for the fellow, but

I've not set eyes on him since he left my office last Tuesday night.'

Inspector Moore looked at his note-book.

'You quarrelled again with him there,' he said. 'You were heard from the street — for a time your door was open, and I am told that you were heard shouting that you would break every bone in his body if he dared come near you again.'

Turner laughed.

'I admit it, but we all say things in a temper. I expect you often remarked that somebody ought to be shot, Inspector, but I don't suppose you exactly meant it.'

'What were you fighting about this time?' snapped Moore.

'An old argument. Morris said that he'd been sent by Mr. Ayres to buy my shed — to make me sell it, as to put me out of business,' Dick answered.

'Is that true, Mr. Ayres?' asked the Inspector.

'I made an offer for the business — a generous offer,' said the mill-owner slowly.

'Yes, very generous,' said Turner. 'So

generous that it was then I told Morris that I'd break him to bits if he dared come near me again.'

'How much did Morris offer you?' asked Blackmore, ignoring the Inspector's frown at the interruption. 'Was it five thousand pounds?'

'What? Not five thousand shillings,' was the reply. 'I wouldn't have sold it, anyway.'

'That question wasn't necessary,' said the Inspector to John Blackmore.

'It is,' insisted the detective, 'and it's the reason why I am here. 'Turner, what exactly was Morris' offer?'

'Two hundred pounds, and the price of the building,' he replied.

Blackmore turned to Jacob Ayres.

'You told Miss Reed you'd sent Morris along with five thousand pounds,' he said. 'If that is so I suggest that your manager has been playing his own game — not yours — and that he worked deliberately for Turner to turn him down.'

'Does that account for you having the auditors at the mill?' said a voice, and they all looked in surprise, for in the excitement of the last few minutes Dr.

Hibbet had been entirely forgotten. 'When you told me you thought something was wrong there I never connected Henry Morris with it.'

'Nor do I, as yet,' snapped Ayres, his colour rising. 'All I'm certain of is that Morris went to this fellow with an offer, and I've no reason to doubt he made it.'

'I've told you the truth,' said Richard Turner. 'Now I'll do all I can to prove that Morris was as crooked as they make 'em. I've had enough of this hole-in-the-corner business. Miss Reed has just told me about how she found this so-called confession of mine among Morris' papers, and how you tried to get it from her. I knew Morris was a blackmailing worm, but I never knew how deeply you were in it with him.' He slapped the document down in front of the scowling man. 'There's your precious confession — now show it to Mr. Blackmore, and I'll take everything that's coming to me.'

Blackmore had noticed that Turner and the girl were whispering a little apart, and was glad that she had told him what had happened.

Jacob Ayres glanced at the paper in front of him.

'I don't know anything about it,' he said in a low voice.

'I heard you say you'd been looking for it,' cut in Cartwright. 'You were trying to steal it from Miss Reed's handbag when I interfered in the hotel.'

'I was going to destroy it,' snapped the old man, and made a grab at the paper.

'It's too late for that now,' said Turner, pinning Ayres' hand to the table. 'Mr. Blackmore is going to be told everything, and then you'll have no further hold on me!'

There was a short struggle for the paper, but the younger man eventually got it, tearing it from the mill-owner's fist.

'I'll break you — break you!' panted Ayres.

He was shaking with rage, and the colour flooded his face until it became an unsightly purple.

'Calm yourself man!' Dr. Hibbet cried in alarm. 'I've warned you of the danger of that temper.'

'Leave me alone!' shouted the old man,

and picking up the liqueur glass drained its contents at a gulp. 'That's — '

His voice broke, and for a moment he stood swaying. Then, tearing at his collar as if it was choking him, he uttered a deep groan and crashed forward against the table.

Dr. Hibbet hurried to his side, and with the help of Blackmore lifted him back into the chair. But it did not need expert knowledge to tell them that Jacob Ayres was beyond help. He was dead!

3

The Shot in The Night

A tense silence followed that sudden collapse. It seemed impossible that a man could be struck down with such lightning rapidity, and for a moment even Blackmore wondered if they had not made a mistake.

But with Ayres stretched out on the settee the doctor made a more careful examination. He rose from this with a grave face, and shook his head at the silent group.

'He's dead!' he said.

'It doesn't seem possible,' Moore muttered. 'Why, a shot man couldn't have dropped quicker.'

'I've warned Ayres many times,' said the doctor. 'Too full blooded. Too quick tempered. It's a dangerous combination at his age.'

'You mean he's had a fit?' asked the Inspector.

'Yes,' said the doctor. 'Though I'll admit I've seldom seen a man go down so quickly. Apoplexy does take some that way, though.'

'You're quite sure it was apoplexy?' John Blackmore asked quietly.

The doctor looked at him angrily.

'I know my business, Mr. — er — Mr. Blackmore.' He said. 'What do you mean?'

'Nothing. Nothing,' said the detective.

But everyone in the room was watching him. Ignoring the doctor's question he had picked up a clean glass and was squeezing the cloth which had become soaked from the contents of the liqueur bottle, which, in his fall, Jacob Ayres had knocked over. He managed to extract seven or eight drops of the amber liquid, and stared at the little pool thoughtfuly.

'What are you doing?' asked the doctor.

'Why — ' and then a sudden light broke in on him. 'Are you trying to suggest that he was poisoned?'

'I'm not suggesting anything,' said the detective. 'But Mr. Ayres drank from that glass a moment before he died. Unfortunately he also smashed the bottle which held the liqueur. I think, doctor, that you had better take charge of the bottle.'

'Ridiculous!' snapped the doctor. 'I've known Ayres for some years. I've warned him repeatedly that he'd go out from heart failure or apoplexy. I know of no poison that could strike a man down so quickly.'

'But doctor, there are poisons that you and I know very little about.'

'Not so many!' snapped Dr. Hibbet. 'Anyway, I'll have no hesitation in certifying that he died of natural causes!'

Blackmore was peering closely at the empty and broken bottle.

'H'm,' he said. 'Armantillo. Very uncommon liqueur. Was Mr. Ayres in the habit of drinking this?'

'He's done so for years,' answered Hibbet. 'Has it sent from London. It's ridiculous to suggest that there could have been anything wrong with it!'

Blackmore slowly turned the bottle, even tilting it to examine the base. Then he held it up to the light, but evidently failed to find what he was looking for.

'Inspector Moore, I must ask you to

take charge of this bottle,' he said quietly. 'I have no wish to go against your professional judgment, doctor, but the manner of Mr. Ayres' death needs investigating. It reminds me of a series of strange deaths that have interested me for some time.'

Harry Cartwright opened his eyes, and looked at his employer.

'You mean the Daniels will case?' he asked.

'That for one — and there are some others,' answered Blackmore, and he looked across at the Inspector.

'Do you remember the death of Felton Daniels, the Liverpool shipowner, Moore?' he asked.

'H'm! I remember he died very suddenly and there was — '

'Exactly,' said the detective. 'He died when he was on the point of signing a new will — a change that would have cut out a distant cousin, and have benefited the Liverpool charities enormously. The cousin who inherited disappeared within a month. He has not been seen since, though half of Daniels' fortune went with him!'

'But what has all this got to do with the death of Mr. Ayres?' asked Dr Hibbet impatiently.

'Only that Daniels collapsed with apoplexy as sudden as Ayres did — and as others have done within the last year,' replied Blackmore. 'I've kept a record of these sudden fatalities — a grim list, doctor.'

'If you'll glance through my books you'll find a grimmer one, for sudden death is no uncommon complaint in this country,' said Hibbet. 'If you've any medical knowledge, Blackmore, you must recognise the cause of Ayres' death — the congestion of the neck, the flooding of blood to the face, the purple tinge in the ear-tips. No, sir, as a doctor I say that the cause was apoplexy!' He turned to the Inspector. 'Mr. Ayres had informed me that his son, Jim, is due in the London docks to-night. He is home from the East, and a sad welcome he'll have after being away for so many years. The news will have to be broken to him, Moore.'

'I'll see to that, doctor,' said the Inspector. He looked down at the old mill-owner for a moment and then turned away. 'Turner, I'm sorry I brought you up here, but I'm bound to go through with the job now. We had better go back to your shed, for there are a few questions I should like to ask you about Morris.'

'I'm as anxious for him to be found as you are,' said that young man.

John Blackmore picked up the glass that held the few drops of liqueur and followed the others from the room. A whisper to Cartwright had sent the secretary ahead, and when the detective reached the car, he was unstrapping the leather case that was always with them. Quickly he hauled out a four inch test tube.

'Switch on the lights,' ordered Blackmore quietly. 'There's not much of the stuff and we mustn't lose a drop of it.'

Standing full in the glare, and facing the car, he held up the tube and tilted the glass.

Phis-s-s!

Something whizzed past Blackmore's face! A bell-like note tinkled on the glass, the rim remained between his fingers, but the lower half shattered to a thousand fragments on the path at his feet!

With great presence of mind Cartwright realised what had happened and switched off the lights.

'That was an air-gun shot!' he said. 'Could it have been meant for you?'

'Quiet!' Blackmore ordered, listening intently and staring into the black shrubbery that bordered the drive.

But not a sound broke the stillness, and it was impossible to guess from whence the shot had come. Unfortunately everyone had been staring at the glass Blackmore held, and the car's lights had practically blinded them for the time being.

'That fellow wasn't firing at me,' said the detective softly. 'I remember the blinds were not drawn in that dining-room — somebody has been watching us the whole of the time, and it was the destruction of the glass he wanted. Look after that bottle, Moore, and if I call come after me.'

Slipping out of sight behind the car John Blackmore skirted the house and made his way through the shrubbery silently. But there was nothing to be found, and he returned to the group who were anxiously waiting his return.

'No luck,' he said. 'That man is a good shot, Moore, but not quite quick enough.'

'Too damn quick, to my idea,' said the Inspector. 'He's destroyed your evidence — if it was evidence.'

'It was, and is,' said the detective. 'He destroyed the glass, but a second after I had transferred the liqueur into the tube! Take care of it, Cartwright, we'll have a look at it when we get back to Dipton.'

Blackmore invited Mary Reed to sit in the front of the car with him, and the others crowded into the back. Under cover of the noise from the engine Blackmore began to talk to the girl quietly.

'Do you know the housekeeper at Mr. Morris' place?' he asked.

'Yes Mrs. Cheen. I often went there with papers from the office,' answered the girl.

'Do you think she'd let you have a look round his rooms?'

'I think she would, if she knows we are trying to find him,' said Mary Reed. 'But what's the good of going there — if he'd returned we would have heard of it, Mr. Blackmore.'

'I don't think he will return,' said the detective. 'But I want you to search his room before anyone else does,' Blackmore explained. His voice dropped still lower, and the girl's eyes opened in amazement as she listened to him. 'Don't say a word to Moore, and when we get to Dipton make an excuse for not coming along to the shed.'

As it happened the Inspector himself asked Blackmore to stop the car, and paved the way for the girl to leave them.

'You might stop at the station, Mr. Blackmore,' he called. 'I'll ask the sergeant to phone London about Jim Ayers. They can tell him what's happened and ask him to hurry home.' As he got down from the car he turned to Miss Reed. 'After that shot in the dark, Miss, I'm not making up my mind over-quickly about what's happened to Morris. No need for you to come along to Mr.

Turner's shed, there'll be nothing doing to-night.'

'If you're sure you won't want me — ' began Mary.

'No, I shan't want you. Go home, and don't talk too much at the works to-morrow,' said Moore briskly. 'Shan't keep you a moment, Mr. Blackmore.'

Dick Turner was looking at Mary Reed questioningly.

'It's all right,' smiled Blackmore. 'Miss Reed is not deserting you, she's going to do something for me.'

'It's all right, Mr. Blackmore,' he said. 'I'm only sorry she has been dragged into this business at all. I can't thank you enough, Mary, for bringing Mr. Blackmore here, but it is the expense — '

'Don't let that worry you at present,' said the detective. 'I've an idea that this is leading to a big affair. Anyway, Miss Reed didn't ask me to come. My secretary butted in on her trouble.'

The young man looked relieved. He had been wondering what he should say to the famous detective. The development of his two colour process had taken every spare penny he had.

'I knew Morris was a scamp, Mr. Blackmore,' he said, after a pause. 'I'm beginning to wonder if he wasn't worse than I thought.'

'He certainly doesn't seem too nice a gentleman,' said Blackmore. 'But here's Moore back. Off you go, Miss Reed.'

The girl nodded, and was out of sight by the time the Inspector reached the car. Harry Cartwright wondered why his employer had sent the girl to do a job for him. Why couldn't he have gone? This girl was a perfect stranger. But he knew better than to put the question to the detective, and remained silent until they reached the weaving shed.

'If you'll come to the office first, I'll tell you exactly what passed between Morris and I on Tuesday night,' said Turner as he got out of the car. 'Then you can search the place until you're tired, but you won't find anything there.'

Opening the door he saw Bill Dale.

'Hello, Bill! I'm glad you're here. You'll be able to bear out what I'm going to say about Morris.'

'I can tell you right now — he was a no good 'un!' growled Bill Dale.

'If you don't mind, Turner,' said Inspector Moore, 'I'll have that paper you were arguing about with Mr. Ayres.'

'Here it is,' said Turner, passing the paper to him. 'And when you've read it I'll tell you how Morris got it from me.'

The Inspector glanced at the signed confession and looked up with a frown.

'Doesn't matter how he got it, it seems to me to prove that you had good reason to hate and fear him,' he snapped. 'However, what about this five thousand pound offer he was supposed to come to you with?'

'As I told Ayres, Morris offered me two hundred — and even that was offered in such a way that I'm certain it was only made to stir up a quarrel,' Dick Turner answered quietly. 'Anyway, I was telling him to clear out when Bill Dale came in from the shed to say some more stuff was ruined — an acid had been dropped into bales of our finished goods, and I may as well tell you that it wasn't the first time that had happened.'

'You mean that it was done deliberately?' asked Blackmore.

'It was that, mister,' broke in Bill Dale. 'I said all along that Morris was bribing somebody to ruin the lad's business — so that he could buy him out cheap, the rat!'

'And Bill told him so to his face,' said Turner. 'Morris blazed out, and it ended up with me saying I'd ring his neck if he didn't leave my affairs alone.'

'So there was no mention made of the five thousand pounds?' demanded Moore.

'There was not!' replied Dick Turner. 'Though I wouldn't sell this process for double that. Anyway, Morris finally cleared out of here, about eight-forty-five, swearing he'd have the place in his hands within one month.'

'And you haven't seen him since?' said the Inspector.

'Nor likely to,' the young man replied. 'You heard Mr. Ayres admit there was something wrong at his works, and you'll find that Morris was up to his neck — What was that?'

The office door suddenly banged open

and something fell inward with a thud. Inspector Moore, nearest the door, turned sharply, and gave a gasp of surprise as he recognised the still form lying on the floor!

4

The Print on The Windscreen

'It's Morris!' shouted Inspector Moore. 'Turner, what does this mean? What game are you playing?'

But Blackmore and his secretary never heard the reply. They were determined to find the key to this second Dipton mystery, and while Moore was speaking they had darted from the office and were staring up and down the dark street.

'There's not a soul in sight, and not a sound,' said Cartwright. 'But Morris couldn't have put himself there.'

But one part of the mystery was quickly solved. From the direction of Jacob Ayres' mill came the sound of a high-powered car engine springing to life.

Blackmore and Cartwright automatically jumped into their own car and threw in the clutch. But there was no answering roar from the big grey machine, and they realised that it had been tampered with.

Cartwright looked down.

'The tyres are flat,' he said.

'And the connection is cut,' answered the detective. He sprang from behind the wheel. 'Come on!' he said, and together they raced down the street.

As they rounded the corner they saw the tail light of a swiftly disappearing car.

'It's no good,' panted Harry. 'There they go. Can't even see how many are in it, or what make it is. They've got the laugh on us.'

There was every excuse for his disgust, for it was seldom that these two were so completely outwitted. The shadowy blur of the car raced round a far corner and in a second had gone, leaving only a roaring drone that toned quickly down to utter silence.

'They've certainly been too quick for us. It seems a desperate game. They must have wrecked our machine the moment we entered Turner's shed.'

'But what was the idea of pitching Morris in like that?' asked the secretary. 'Don't see the sense of it. They mightn't have had the luck to get away so quickly.'

'I don't think they intended Morris to be found so quickly,' said the detective. 'The door couldn't have been properly fastened, and the weight of the body burst it open.'

'What about our car? They might have left some trace there of who they are.'

'We'll attend to Morris first,' said Blackmore.

Entering the office again they found Inspector Moore questioning Turner as if he had actually caught him in the act of killing Morris.

'It's no good you saying you know nothing about it, Turner,' Moore was saying. 'He disappears from your office — and he's found on your doorstep. If you haven't done the job yourself you must have a good idea who has — '

'Are you mad, Inspector?' interrupted Turner sharply. 'If I'd had anything to do with it do you think I'd have been such a fool as to bring him here under your nose like this?'

'He was brought here by some persons who have just got away in a racing car,' said Blackmore quietly. 'No good you rushing out now, Moore. We only caught a glimpse of the car, and they have put ours out of action. Morris is dead, I suppose?'

One glance was enough to convince them, though there was no trace of injury on him. He lay there as if sleeping, but when Blackmore touched his face it was icy cold.

'H'm! He's been dead for several hours!' he muttered. 'Do you notice anything, Moore?'

The Inspector looked and then shook his head.

'Nothing, except that he's dead,' he said.

'He has the same flushed appearance that Ayres had,' said the detective. 'It's almost as if the same thing had killed them both.'

'I'm still to be convinced that Ayres didn't come to a natural end,' said the Inspector stubbornly. 'Anyway, this is a police job — you'd better keep away from Morris until the police surgeon has examined him.'

'I'm not disturbing him,' said Blackmore quietly. The Inspector was an irritating man, but he knew he must keep his temper. 'Do you see this — looks like a pin-prick that has inflamed the flesh all round it.'

Now that Blackmore had pointed it out they could see an angry spot behind the left ear — a purple centre, surrounded by reddish skin that gradually faded to the natural colour.

'Point that out to your doctor when he comes,' said the detective.

'But what does it all mean, Mr. Blackmore?' asked the bewildered Turner. 'I somehow seem to be mixed up in the deaths of both these men. But I'll swear that I never had anything more to do with them than ask them to leave me alone.'

'I don't know what it means, Turner,' said John Blackmore. 'But it seems as if Morris has been playing a tricky game, and has paid for it with his life.'

The 'phone bell rang and Bill Dale picked up the receiver. After a second or two he called over:

'It's for you, Inspector, from the station,' he said.

'Tell them to send a doctor and a couple of men along at once,' snapped the Inspector. 'Do you know, Blackmore, I'm getting the jumps over this job. I can see a dozen reasons why Turner could have had a hand in it, and he's an ass if he thinks he can bluff me with this fancy ending. I can tell you, young fellow,' he said, turning to Dick, 'this is a coroner's case, and you'll have some awkward questions to answer.'

'I know no more than I've told you,' said the young man. 'I'm as puzzled as you are as to why Morris should have been dumped on my doorstep.'

'That's plain enough,' said Harry Cartwright. 'I'd say he had been killed a good many miles from here, and by somebody who knew how you hated each other. It isn't an easy thing to get rid of a body, so they would naturally place it where it would draw suspicion away from them.'

John Blackmore smiled.

'Before your doctor comes, Moore, we'd better have a look at my car.'

A quick examination showed that the

45

valves of all four tyres had been loosened, and the tyres were flat. The petrol tank was empty and the magneto smashed. In all a very determined way of seeing that they could not be pursued once they had got away.

'Hello!' cried Cartwright suddenly. 'Somebody's been handling the windscreen — leaning over to get at the magneto box. And look, Mr. Blackmore, he's left a thumb-print that would gladden any detective's heart. See it?'

Even to the unpractised eye of Turner and Bill Dale, the print stood out startlingly clear, though they wondered how anybody could be traced by a smudge. Moore alone was inclined to belittle the secretary's find.

'It may have been there for days,' he said.

'Don't you believe it,' said Harry. 'It was raining hard until an hour ago.'

'Then it was probably left by one of the fellows when you garaged it at the hotel,' snapped Moore.

'And probably not!' snapped the secretary. 'I wiped the windscreen myself when I put it away.'

During this conversation Cartwright had been rummaging in the car. He knew very well what would be wanted. And while Blackmore was adjusting a pocket Kodak, he brought out a wide-mouthed pistol and a tray, in which he poured a generous quantity of grey powder.

'All right,' said Blackmore. 'Not too close.'

'Right!' said the secretary, pointing the pistol about six inches from the glass.

There was a dull plop, and a stream of yellow powder shot forth and settled in a thick film over the corner of the screen. Blowing at it gently he soon dispersed most of the powder, leaving only a heavy, well outlined crust on the thumb-print.

'Now the flare,' said the detective.

As the magnesium powder blazed in a brilliant blue flare the detective snapped off three negatives.

'Would you let me have a copy of those photographs?' asked the Inspector. 'I don't think my men could better your methods.'

'Of course,' answered the detective. 'You can have them to-morrow. I can guess what happened, Moore, when the fellow was letting down the tyres he must have got some oil on his hands, and in leaning over gave this beauty.'

'Then if he's an old 'lag' we've got him,' said the Inspector importantly.

'I'll be surprised if he is,' said the detective. 'This doesn't seem like ordinary crook work. The death of a mill-owner and his manager in one night seems strange to me.' He looked up as footsteps sounded on the gravel. 'I think these are your men.'

Three men came into the light of the car, two constables and a lean-faced man, who was obviously the police surgeon.

'Wish you'd have your troubles at a more convenient time, Moore,' growled the doctor. 'What is it this time, a factory accident?'

'More serious than that, Foley,' replied Inspector Moore. 'It's Mr. Morris, of the big mill. You heard he's been missing for some days? He's in Turner's office, dead!' He smiled grimly at the suspicious look the doctor gave to Turner.

'All right, but must we have a crowd?' said Dr. Foley. 'You'd better come in,

Turner, and — who is this?' he snapped, looking at John Blackmore.

Inspector Moore introduced the detective and his secretary, and the doctor's eyes opened when he heard the name, but did not show any surprise.

'Get busy on the car, Harry,' said the detective. 'Perhaps Dale will help you?'

'I don't know much about car engines,' said the foreman, 'but I'll do whatever you say.'

They went into the shed. The doctor's examination was brief.

'H'm! Rigor mortis well developed; been dead five to seven hours,' he muttered. 'No sign of injury. If he'd been in bed I'd have said he died of heart failure. H'm! Funny to see Morris with this colour, he was always white-faced. Hello, what's this?'

He looked up with a frown, and pointed to the tiny inflamed spot behind the dead man's ear.

'Looks like a puncture from a hypodermic needle!' he said quickly. 'Have you seen it, Moore?'

'Yes, Mr. Blackmore pointed it out to

49

me,' answered Moore. 'What do you make of it?'

'Injection of some sort, dangerously near the brain,' Foley replied. 'Well, I can do nothing more here. It will mean an inquest, of course. I suppose you are waiting to go through his pockets?'

Moore nodded, but the search brought them very little result. A few business letters, a watch, keys and so on. In one pocket they found a tiny bottle labelled 'Toothache Tincture.'

'Oh, he had tooth trouble,' murmured the doctor, and looking at the bottle. 'Not that this stuff would do him any good.'

'It wouldn't,' said Blackmore quietly. 'Wouldn't help him at all, he's got a complete set of false teeth!'

Foley looked again at the dead man.

'So he has. Then what the devil does he want to carry 'Tooth Tincture' with him for?'

Taking out the cork the doctor found that except for a few drops the bottle was empty. Sniffing it he murmured something about 'iodoform,' and was going to put the tip of his tongue on the cork when

Blackmore snatched the bottle from his hand.

'Sorry, Foley,' he said, 'but I've an idea that that stuff isn't toothache remedy. Moore, put this with the others I gave you, and take care of it, it might be a great help.'

Foley frowned, but the Inspector ordered the men to remove the body, and he allowed the matter to drop. With the removal of the body the doctor left them. When the three men were alone Moore turned sourly to Turner.

'I'm not at all satisfied,' he said. 'We don't know yet how Morris died, but there's still the matter of the five thousand pounds missing, and we all know how hard up you are. You had better come along to the station with me now. And I tell you frankly, Turner, I'm going to have a search warrant.'

'You've no need to do that,' said Dick Turner, his face flushing. 'Here's the keys of the safe and the desk. You can search every inch of the place if you like.'

'I'm going to,' answered Moore shortly. 'Are you coming with me, Mr. Blackmore?'

'No, thank you,' said the detective. 'I'm going back to the hotel. I'll be glad if you'll tell me where I can knock up a chemist.'

The Inspector gave the information with a curling lip.

'Want a sleeping draught, I suppose,' he said bitingly. 'Lucky man, we poor devils in the force are not allowed to sleep when we like.'

'Nor allowed to think as you like, eh, Moore?' smiled the detective. 'You're bound down by copy-book rules, but the men you hunt don't always work to copy-book methods.'

He nodded to Turner, and was out of the office before the Inspector could reply. The man had irritated him badly, and the last thing he wanted to do was to create ill-feeling between them.

The Inspector would have been considerably surprised and mystified had he followed Blackmore's movements during the next couple of hours.

5

The Almost Perfect Murder

It was nearly midnight when John Blackmore and Harry Cartwright returned to the Dipton Hotel. They were loaded with parcels bought from a nearby chemist, and they had had great difficulty in getting the particular things they were requiring.

A discreet tip to the porter gave them the use of the pantry as a dark-room, and their private sitting-room was soon turned into a makeshift laboratory.

'You develop those negatives, Harry,' said the detective, 'and I'll try and find out what this liqueur is composed of.'

'All right,' said the secretary. 'It won't take me long to do that, and I want to watch you work on the test.'

Alone, John Blackmore quickly unwrapped the bottles he had brought from the chemist and placed them in a handy row on the table in front of him. He had been fortunate in being able to get a Bunsen burner, a length of rubber tubing and some padded aluminium pincers.

From his waistcoat pocket he brought out the test-tube containing the few drops of liquor squeezed from the cloth in the dining room of Ayres' home. The hotel still used gas for their lighting system, for which Blackmore was grateful, otherwise he would have had to return to Town before he could complete the test.

The rubber tubing had been fixed to the gas bracket, and he was ready to start when Cartwright burst into the room.

'Fine copies, Mr. Blackmore,' he said with excitement. 'If the owner of these is in the 'Rogues' gallery he's as good as ours.'

He watched Blackmore carefully tilt half the amber drops into a spare test tube.

'I'm curious to know if that drink was doped,' he said. 'Though I can't see that any dope would put a man out like that.'

'As far as I know there's only one poison that can do it,' said the detective. 'I'm testing for that now. Turn the light a little this way, thanks. Give me those pincers, and then light the burner.'

Cartwright did as directed, and then watched the operation. For some time the detective worked, heating this tube, adding a little water, here, and something from another bottle there. After a while, with the result in one tube, the detective turned to his secretary with a grim face.

'I was right,' he said quietly. 'There will have to be a more elaborate test at the Home Office, that was why I halved what little I had, but the little I have been able to find out has proved that Ayres was poisoned.'

'Was it a rare poison?' asked the secretary.

'Not so rare,' said the detective, but he did not explain the nature of it.

'But poisoning is out of date,' protested Cartwright. 'You don't mean to say that a clever crook would try that sort of game nowadays?'

'I mean to say that you witnessed the almost perfect murder, young man,' answered Blackmore grimly. 'You heard Dr. Hibbet say that he has warned Ayres many times against excitement — that he was convinced that he died of apoplexy?'

'But he's not the first doctor to make a mistake,' said Cartwright. 'He was bound to have found it out when he made a closer examination.'

'There wouldn't have been one; he had attended Ayres for years,' said the detective. 'I don't blame him for making a mistake. The peculiarity of this poison is that it gives the victim the exact appearance of having died from apoplexy!'

'How did you ever guess at this?' asked the secretary.

'Two things helped me,' Blackmore answered. 'The first was that Ayres collapsed the moment after draining his glass, and that as he fell clutched at his throat as though something burned him. The second was the memory of those other sudden deaths that rich men have lately suffered from.'

Cartwright whistled.

'You mean there's a poisoning gang loose murdering for what they can make out of it?'

'Yes,' said the detective. 'They are clever, they pick only carefully selected victims, that's the main point.'

'It's queer, though,' mused the secretary. 'We stop off here, a little Midland work-centre, and drop clean into a murder case.'

'Don't forget Morris,' said his employer. 'He turned up — and if I've not made a mistake we'll find that he was murdered, too.' He was silent as Cartwright cleared away the things he had been using. 'The connection is clear enough to a point,' he went on. 'But there's a break. We've got to find how Morris spent those three days when he was missing.'

'And we've got to find out how that stuff got into the bottle of liqueur,' said Cartwright. 'I should think it was a servant in the house. It must have been someone who knew the doctor was coming, and then killed him in such a way that the doctor would say that he had been expecting it.'

'I don't think so,' said the detective. 'If that was the case it must have been a servant with an amazing knowledge of science. That was pure nicotine, refined and refined until it reaches a state of maximum purity, and that gives you one of the most deadly poisons known. No, Harry, I don't think it was a servant.'

He looked at his watch.

'It's nearly two o'clock, what about bed?' he said.

'I'm ready,' said the secretary. 'I suppose you've made up your mind to stay here? You haven't said anything about getting back to town.'

'We'll be staying for a time,' smiled the detective, and turned out the light.

At breakfast next morning Inspector Moore came into the room, scowling as though he was suffering from indigestion.

''Morning,' he snapped. 'Nice thing happened in the night, Blackmore. Men on duty locked in their room, the sergeant knocked on the head. Nice thing for me, isn't it?'

Harry Cartwright laughed heartily.

'Gosh! that's great! Burglars in the police station!'

'Is that right?' asked Blackmore.

'What else!' growled Moore. 'Safe

toppled over, the back of it burnt out like sliced cheese, and all for a rotten bit of glass!'

'What!' gasped Cartwright. 'Have you let 'em pinch that bottle?'

'Has the bottle really gone?' asked the detective.

'That's what I'm trying to tell you,' groaned the Inspector. 'I didn't think much of your suspicions, but I locked the bottle up as you asked, and now I'll be the laughing stock of the town.'

Blackmore was silent for a moment.

'I ought to have foreseen a move like this,' he said at last. 'It's clear enough now — whoever watched me squeezing that tablecloth must have seen me hand you the bottle.'

'And when they shot the glass from your hand they never knew you had the stuff already in the tube,' said Cartwright. 'They'd think they only had to steal the bottle to completely destroy the evidence.'

'I don't believe there is any evidence,' snarled Moore. 'I'm not very popular among the toughs of Dipton, and they've played this game to make me look a fool. Stealing an empty bottle! Hell, I'll get it from the Super when he hears of this.'

'Ever heard of nicotine, Moore?' asked Blackmore, casually.

'What's that got to do with it?' asked the angry Inspector. 'Of course I've heard of nicotine, what do you mean?'

'I mean that Jacob Ayres died of nicotine poisoning, and that it came from that bottle,' answered the detective quietly. 'We've already tested that stuff that I squeezed from the cloth. It was strongly impregnated with nicotine, and two drops of that means certain death!'

The Inspector sat down at the table with a gasp.

'Great Scott, Blackmore!' he muttered. 'But who would want to kill old Jacob Ayres? There's only that one son to inherit the money, and Jim hasn't been near the country for getting on twenty years.'

'Didn't you say he was arriving last night?' asked Cartwright.

'Get that idea out of your head,' said the Inspector. 'The boat didn't dock until nearly midnight — and Jim Ayres has a cast iron alibi if anyone says he has a hand in it.'

'But we're not accusing him, Moore,' said Blackmore. 'What was the result of searching Turner's shed?'

'There wasn't a thing,' replied the Inspector. 'Might have guessed there wouldn't be when you hopped off so quickly. But I still think he's got a lot to explain about Morris.'

'And I'm certain Ayres could have explained more,' said John Blackmore. 'You must have noticed that Ayres had no wish to speak of Morris at all. And if he was speaking the truth about Morris having five-thousand of his, why didn't he report the fellow's disappearance before?'

Inspector Moore stroked his chin thoughtfully.

'If only we knew where Morris spent the time between Tuesday and last night,' he said.

'That's what we've got to find out,' said Blackmore quickly. 'His jumping off point was Ayres' house, and I've an idea the old man said something to him that sent him off in a panic. We are going to the house now and see if the butler can tell us anything. You'd better come along, Moore.'

'I can't,' said the Inspector. 'The papers are full of the case, and the Chief wants me at ten — he phoned.'

'You'll have to tell him about our nicotine discovery, but see that no one else gets to know of it, Moore,' said the detective. 'You understand? Once that news gets out we are lost!'

'You don't have to tell me that,' said the Inspector. 'By the way,' he went on. 'I had a report from Dr. Foley. He says Morris was killed by some unknown poison injected with a hypodermic needle.'

'Thanks, Moore, I'm not surprised to hear it,' said Blackmore. 'Have you fixed the inquest yet?'

'To-morrow, at ten,' said the Inspector. 'The auditors at the mill have been asking me the same question.'

'I expect so,' said the detective dryly.

Fifteen minutes later Blackmore and Cartwright were speeding up the drive of Ayres' house. Their knock was answered by the butler, Thomson, an old white-haired man, shaken and nervous with the shock of his master's sudden death.

'I would like to speak to you privately, Thomson,' said the detective. 'It's about Mr. Morris' visit here last Tuesday.'

'Yes, Mr. Blackmore,' said the old butler. 'Come in, sir,' he said, glancing nervously over his shoulder as he spoke.

He hurried them across the hall and into the room where Jacob Ayres had died the night before. He seemed anxious to get them in, and closed the door so quietly that Cartwright wondered if he wanted their visit kept secret.

'Mr. Blackmore, I heard you talking to the doctor last night,' he began. 'You — you seemed to think the master had — hadn't died naturally.'

'Well?' asked Blackmore, eyeing the old man closely.

'Do you still think that, sir?' Thomson stammered.

'I do!' said the detective. 'Mr. Ayres was poisoned.'

The butler's sallow face turned pale.

'Mr. Blackmore,' he said. 'I was afraid

you'd say that. I'm to blame, sir. You see, the master keeps his special wine in this sideboard cupboard.'

'Yes?'

'Well, sir, one night last week I lost my keys, couldn't find them anywhere,' muttered Thomson. 'They turned up next morning, they were found under this table. But I ought to have told Mr. Ayres they were missing, for somebody must have used my keys to get at that bottle of Armantillo.'

'One moment, perhaps you are blaming yourself unnecessarily,' said Blackmore kindly. 'What night was it you missed the keys?'

'It was on Saturday night, Mr. Blackmore. It was on Sunday morning that the maid found them.'

'Well, now, think carefully, Thomson,' said Blackmore. 'Are you sure Mr. Ayres didn't use the bottle between Saturday and last night?'

Thomson wrinkled his forehead in an effort of concentration.

'Let me see. He dined out on Sunday night. On Monday he drank cognac,' he said slowly. 'Tuesday — why, yes — Tuesday he did have a little of the Armantillo, just a nip, sir. I'd just put the bottle away when Mr. Morris came in.' The strained expression left his face and he gave a nervous smile. 'I've been awake all night, sir,' he said, 'thinking that I'd had a hand in killing the master, as you might say.'

'May I have your keys, Thomson?' asked the detective, and when they were handed over: 'Which is the key of the wine cupboard?'

The old butler pointed out one of the smaller keys, and watched anxiously while the detective first rubbed his thumb slowly along the barrel, then examined the key under a magnifying glass which he had taken from his pocket.

'What do you make of this?' he asked Cartwright, passing the key over to him.

The secretary stared at it for a moment, and then took the glass from his employer's hand. He looked at the key under the glass for a moment and then stared at the detective.

'It feels greasy. And I'd say there had been a wax impression taken of it.' He studied it under the glass again. 'Yes, there's a tiny pin-point of wax still in the barrel.'

Blackmore nodded and handed the key back to the unsuspecting butler.

'Now, Thomson, about Mr. Morris,' he asked. 'Did he often come to the house or was Tuesday's a special visit?'

'Oh, no, sir, he came here two or three nights every week,' answered the butler. 'He'd bring papers from the office, or cheques to be signed. Lately the master had left things in his hands.'

'Do you know why he came on Tuesday?'

'I heard them talking while I was serving the coffee,' said the butler. 'Mr. Ayres was discussing the Turner weaving shed. He said there was a fortune in it. He gave Mr. Morris a packet of bank-notes, and said that Turner would jump at them, seeing the mess he was in.'

'Anything else?' asked Blackmore, as the old man paused.

'Nothing else, sir,' he said. 'I had to go out to the phone in the hall. It was a call for Mr. Ayres, and I told him. He came out and spoke on the phone.'

'And when did Morris leave?'

'Soon afterwards,' said the butler. 'About ten minutes later. When Mr. Ayres rang for me to show him out he was telling Mr. Morris about Master Jim coming home soon. Mr. Morris asked him what boat he was coming on, and he said he was very surprised that Master Jim was returning at last.'

'And that was all you heard?'

'That was all, except that Mr. Ayres said that he was sorry he had been so hard on the lad — and adding something about taking him into the firm,' answered Thomson. 'I was opening the door for Mr. Morris then, and — '

'It's time an old man knew better than to gas about his boss' affairs!'

The door had opened very quietly, and they now saw a coarse, heavily-built man scowling in the opening. He had American written all over him, from the yellow shoes he wore to the horn-rimmed glasses that failed to hide the fury in his eyes.

'I can see there's going to be trouble in this house!' he cried, striding into the room. 'I thought I told you to keep your mouth closed about Morris, and the first thing I find is you cackling about the fellow.' The fire in his eyes turned to a cold menace, and he seemed to tower over the terrified old man. 'I've been reading the paper, and I'd like to know who in Hell gave you permission to broadcast Morris' doings, eh?'

'I'm — I'm sorry, Master James,' Thomson faltered. 'I thought you only meant I hadn't to talk to reporters.'

'Sorry! That cuts no ice with me!' the fellow snarled. His hand shot out and the butler winced with the steely grip that fastened on his shoulder. 'I didn't make conditions — I just told you not to talk, you — '

'But you haven't the right to, in this case,' said Blackmore smoothly, and at the same time removing the hand that gripped the old man. 'If you're Jim Ayres — '

'I am, and owner of this place,' said Ayres. 'Who the devil are you?'

His fist was clenched and drawn back, as if he meant to start trouble, but John

Blackmore just looked straight at him, with a slight smile. Taking a card from his case he passed it over to Jim Ayres.

'I have been asked to go into the disappearance of Morris — ' he began, but was interrupted by a coarse laugh from Ayres.

'Oh, so you're a detective,' he chuckled. Then, with a hoarse shout he called: 'Hi, Jake — Jake Barnes, come and feast your eyes on London's pet sleuth!'

Harry Cartwright looked as if he would like to interfere, but a warning frown from his employer stopped him, though he felt he would burst out if he had to listen to more sneers from this bully.

But they forgot Jim Ayres when they saw the man who answered the call. This man was bigger and uglier than Jim Ayres, and moved as silently and stealthily as a cat. His face was lined and seamed with healed scars. Big as he was, it seemed to Blackmore that there was something sinister in his quiet padding across the room. But his manner seemed wild and harmless enough.

'Say, you're lifting the lid off, ain't

you?' he asked quietly. 'Why tell the world. You wasn't always such a bone-head, Jim.'

There was reproach in Barnes' tone, and Cartwright noticed that his little eyes glinted cold fury at Ayres. What ever silent message passed between them, Ayres certainly simmered down and turned away.

'All right, Jake — I'm a fool,' he said lamely. 'Mr. Blackmore, I'm considerably upset to get this kind of home-coming, after being away for nearly twenty years. First the old man, then Morris, and all this newspaper publicity stuff. Sorry, I've got a bit tough on my travels, and I ain't quite used to decent folks. And I did take you for a nosy newspaper guy. I'll tone down soon.'

He spoke awkwardly, as if choosing every word carefully. He kept throwing nervous glances at Barnes, and the bitter twist of his lips gave him the look of a mongrel that had just received the taste of the boot.

'That's all right, Ayres,' said Black-more, appearing to accept that halting explanation as quite natural. 'The police will be asking Thomson a lot of questions, so there's no harm in him answering a few of mine.'

'Go on, then,' said Jim Ayres. 'Maybe it will put me wise to Morris' little game. Double-crossing quitter, dynamiting the old man's banking account — '

'Who told you that?' asked Blackmore quickly. 'You know more than we do, though we've got good reason to suspect why the auditors are in the mill now — '

'He means — that bunch of dollars Morris took away with him,' said Jake Barnes, before Jim Ayres could speak. 'You mean that, Jim, just what the papers told you, eh?'

'Of course! What else could I know?' Ayres blustered. 'You see, Blackmore, we came up by road last night. Don't know anything except that the old man cashed in, and that Morris took five thousand pounds away with him.'

Whilst Jim Ayres was blundering on, Barnes took Blackmore's card from his fingers and glanced at it. Then he suddenly looked closer, gave a twisted smile, and tore it into pieces. These he threw into the fireplace, and when old Thomson made to gather it up he stopped him.

'No, no, old war-horse,' he smiled, gently turning the butler until he faced them. 'Them little bit's'll do no harm, and I think Mr. Blackmore still wants some information.'

'No, I've finished,' answered the detective, turning to the door. 'Come on, Cartwright, we've a lot to do.'

In turning he placed his back to the two men, and for one second faced his secretary. The quick glance he gave was understood by the secretary, and Blackmore's hand was already on the knob of the door when he swung round, as if belatedly remembering something.

'Oh, there's just one thing, Thomson,' he said. 'Just let me have those keys of yours again.'

'Yes, sir,' said Thomson, handing them to him.

There was a moment's silence as John Blackmore stood in front of the sideboard, the keys dangling in his hand, his head bent in thought. Ayres and Barnes had stiffened to attention, and neither noticed Cartwright moving cautiously to the fireplace. Then, as the young man bent to gather up the torn slips of cardboard, Blackmore suddenly laughed and tossed the keys back to the butler.

'No, it's too silly,' he said loudly. 'For the moment I really had the idea that Morris was killed by something taken from this cupboard.'

He turned again to the two men.

'You will probably learn at the inquest that Mr. Morris was murdered by the injection of some strange poison — I seem to think that this sideboard was connected with his death. But it's only guess work — and silly at that.'

It sounded lame, and the three men stared at him as if they wondered what he was talking about. They had no eye for Cartwright, who knew that the detective was talking purely to cover his movements. In two seconds he had gathered in every bit of card that had escaped the fire. In another second he was standing behind Barnes — just one second before that fellow turned suspiciously to see what had become of him.

Barnes' glance went to the tiled hearth, and he nodded thoughtfully.

'Yes, Mr. Blackmore, perhaps it is only guesswork,' he said slowly. 'But you might guess right some day, and, I've heard it said, that a little knowledge is a dangerous thing.'

'It's led many a man to the nine o'clock drop,' agreed Blackmore pleasantly. 'Well, we'd better be going. I suppose we shall see you at the inquest.'

'Sure thing,' said Ayres. 'Seems to me that Turner's got to explain where that money is hiding.'

'It seems to me,' said the detective slowly, 'that someone's got to explain where Henry Morris has been hiding!'

And Cartwright grinned as he followed his employer from the room, for he was sure that they were leaving two very puzzled men behind.

6

John Blackmore's Evidence

The inquest on Henry Morris took place the following Monday morning, and by now the wildest rumours were floating round the town. It was whispered that Morris had been a desperate man for months past — that he had committed suicide rather than face the charge of embezzlement.

Blackmore and his secretary were seated close to the coroner's table, with Mary Reed and Dick Turner on one side and Inspector Moore on the other. In the back of the building they saw Jim Ayres and his friend, Jake Barnes, whispering, and ignoring the open curiosity of those who now saw the new mill-owner for the first time.

The coroner, primed by the police, made short work of the first witness, Mrs. Cheen, who had expected Morris back to supper at ten o'clock on the night he vanished. Next, the two men who heard Morris quarrelling with Dick Turner, and even Turner himself was asked to stand down after merely swearing that Morris left his office on the Tuesday evening, and that he next saw him, dead, on the Friday. Then Inspector Moore was called.

'Now, Inspector, I understand you were actually searching for Morris on Friday evening?' began the coroner.

'I was, sir, and I found him in a most unusual way,' said the Inspector. 'I had been to Mr. Ayres' house with Turner, and after the death of the old man we returned to Turner's shed to go on with the Morris enquiry. Turner was denying that he knew anything when the door suddenly fell open and Morris himself tumbled in at my feet — dead!'

A shocked gasp came from the packed crowd at the Inspector's statement, but the coroner's glare soon reduced them to silence.

'When Morris fell, had he just expired?' asked the coroner.

'No, sir, he'd been dead for hours, so

Doctor Foley said,' replied the Inspector. 'Somebody had brought him to the door, propped him up against it, and his weight had forced it open.'

'Have you any idea why he was placed there?' asked the coroner.

'No, sir. But Mr. Blackmore said — '

'Mr. Blackmore will give his own evidence.'

'Very well, sir,' answered Moore sullenly.

'Now, have you any idea as to how he came by his death?'

'I'm not a medical man. Dr. Foley will tell you that,' snapped Moore, glad to get his own back.

'You know that is not what I meant, Inspector,' said the coroner quietly. 'Morris was missing from Tuesday till Friday, with five thousand pounds of Mr. Ayres' money. That money is still missing. Please give me any information you have about it, also anything you can tell me of Morris' three absent days.'

'As to the money, sir, I can only say that Mr. Ayres swore Morris had it, and that Turner and Morris are known to have quarrelled over it,' replied Moore.

'We didn't — we quarrelled over an offer of two hundred pounds he made for my business,' cried Dick Turner, springing to his feet.

'Sit down, sir!' barked the coroner. 'Another interruption and I shall have you ejected from the court.'

'But he's wilfully twisting — ' began Dick hotly.

'You will have an opportunity for answering that if it is necessary,' said the coroner, and turning to the Inspector, 'Please, Inspector, about those three missing days.'

'We have been able to trace that to some extent,' answered Moore. 'Yesterday's enquiries through the newspapers, brought us a reply, late last night. His photograph was recognised by a booking clerk at Heston Airport. He said that Morris booked a seat on the Paris 'plane for Friday morning, paid for his ticket, but never claimed the seat. It was booked in the name of Wilkins, and the address given was false.'

'Which means that he was trying to get

out of the country,' suggested the coroner.

'Yes,' said Moore. 'The auditors at the mill will be able to give you a reason for that.'

The coroner consulted his papers.

'H'm! There's no need to make a secret of that. There is a great deal of money missing, and Morris alone had access to the cheque books,' he said. 'Have you any further information as to how he spent the three days?'

'No, sir. He booked that seat on the Thursday afternoon, and we've no proof of his movements after that.'

The coroner frowned.

'No proof? What does that mean exactly?'

'Well, sir, we cannot bring forward anybody who will swear to having seen Morris from Thursday onward,' Moore answered. 'But Mr. Blackmore was working with me yesterday, and I think we can show that Morris was not very far away.'

'That's cool!' whispered Cartwright to the detective. 'We can prove! Fat lot he had to do with it!'

'Jake Barnes seems to be interested,' answered Blackmore. 'He's wondering what Moore is going to say next.'

But Moore had nothing more to say. The coroner unexpectedly ordered him to stand down.

The next to be called was Dr. Foley.

'I was called in to examine the body of Henry Morris at nine fifty-five on Friday evening,' he said, going straight to the point. 'He had then been dead for five or six hours. The cause of his death was an injection of pure nicotine, forced into his neck by a hypodermic needle.'

'H'm! An uncommon poison, I think,' said the coroner, glaring round the court for silence. 'How would you say he came by his wound, Dr. Foley?'

'I wouldn't hazard a guess,' said the doctor. 'He could quite easily have inflicted it on himself — and anyone else could as easily have done it to him.'

'H'm! That is very unsatisfactory. It means that you will not give an opinion as to whether he committed suicide or whether he was murdered?'

'On the evidence available it is impossible to give an opinion,' said the doctor.

And not all the questioning from the coroner could force the police doctor to alter that vague statement.

When John Blackmore was called a ripple of excitement stirred the audience.

'Mr. Blackmore, I think you have something to tell us concerning the movements of the deceased,' began the coroner quietly. 'But first, I should like it made clear as to why you are in this case when the police already have it in hand?'

'I came into this case to help clear Richard Turner of an unjust suspicion,' answered Blackmore briefly. 'In doing so I will prove that Henry Morris first absconded from Dipton, then returned to try and prevent a murder.'

'What — what do you mean?' gasped the coroner, and for once ignored the whispering that was going on round him.

'I mean that murder of Jacob Ayres,' said Blackmore.

'That's rot! Jacob Ayres was not murdered! He died of apoplexy!'

It was Jim Ayres on his feet, his face flushed with anger, his fist clenched with overpowering rage.

'So that's why you came spying round the house,' he shouted. 'Can't even let the dead rest. Mr. Coroner, this is an enquiry into the death of Morris. I protest against my father's name being brought into it.'

The court was silent. The outburst had left everybody amazed.

'Is it necessary, Mr. Blackmore?' asked the coroner. 'Will it help us in the matter of Morris' death?'

'It will,' answered the detective. 'It will also show that Morris has been the catspaw for people more clever than himself.'

'Very well, you may continue.' And as Jim Ayres jumped up again! 'You must sit down, sir, or leave the court. Mr. Blackmore, you have made an amazing statement. You say that Mr. Ayres was murdered and that Morris returned to Dipton to try and prevent that murder.'

'That is so.'

'Then perhaps you will tell us who killed Mr. Ayres?'

'I can! He was murdered by Henry Morris!'

For a moment there was silence, and then whispering and smothered laughter broke out. But not for long. Nobody took the risk of being removed from the court when there was such amazing information to be had.

'Mr. Blackmore,' said the coroner, 'are you serious? Do you realise that Mr. Ayres died half an hour before the body of Morris was found, and that Dr. Foley has sworn that Henry Morris had been dead for at least five hours?'

'That is so. Henry Morris killed Jacob Ayres five hours after he was dead himself!'

The coroner stared. This was too much for him, but knowing the reputation Blackmore had he knew there must be something in it.

'Mr. Blackmore,' he said quietly. 'Perhaps you had better tell this in your own way. I must confess it is beyond me.'

'I was in the room when Mr. Ayres collapsed,' began the detective, 'and for a moment I never doubted that he had died of apoplexy. In falling over the table Mr. Ayres upset a bottle of liqueur. The widening pool on the cloth reminded me that he had been drinking the stuff before he dropped. I was able to squeeze about ten drops of the liqueur from the cloth. An analysis proved that it was impregnated with nicotine, the poison that also killed Henry Morris.'

John Blackmore paused, and his glance rested on Dr. Hibbet, old Jacob Ayres' own medical advisor.

'I wish it to be understood that Dr. Hibbet cannot be blamed in any way for thinking that his patient had died of apoplexy. Nicotine poison gives exactly the same appearance to its victims, and Hibbet had been treating Mr. Ayres for this complaint for several months. Had I not been suspicious from other causes I would never had doubted his diagnosis.'

Dr. Hibbet nodded and smiled at the detective's generous words.

'I would like to say that Mr. Blackmore has convinced me that he is right, and that several drops of the liqueur have been sent to the public analyst,' he said in an aside to the coroner.

The coroner nodded.

'And you say that Henry Morris committed this crime when he was already dead?' he exclaimed. 'Can you prove that, Mr. Blackmore.'

'Inspector Moore has already told you that Morris had been robbing the Ayres business of vast sums of money,' the detective continued. 'He probably would have gone on doing so for years, and Mr. Ayres would have been alive now, but for the chance that the son, Jim Ayres, decided to come home after many years' absence.

'When Ayres mentioned that fact to Morris he signed his own death warrant. He told him that he intended to make his son a partner in the firm, and Morris must have instantly realised that that would mean a close auditing of the books, and his own exposure.'

He glanced at Jim Ayres, and then turned to the coroner.

'From that moment Morris must have schemed to get the old man out of the way, knowing that Jim Ayres would be without any knowledge of the spinning business, and guessing that affairs would be left in his hands. I have no idea how he obtained the poison, but I will show you the method he used to effect his purpose.'

He then explained his call on the butler, and Thomson's story of the mislaid keys.

'That was last Saturday week, Mr. Coroner,' he said. 'Thomson lost the keys because Morris picked them up, took a wax impression of the wine cupboard key, and slipped the bunch under the table.'

John Blackmore pointed to the things on the coroner's table — Henry Morris' keys, the 'toothache tincture,' and other things that had been found on him.

'On that key-ring you will find a key fitting the wine cupboard at Mr. Ayres' house, and that tiny phial still holds enough poison to kill a dozen people,' he said. 'The butler's keys, now in the possession of Inspector Moore, still show a spot of wax — left by Morris when he took the impression.

'That brings us to the Tuesday night when Morris vanished. The butler will tell you that Morris received a roll of bank-notes and was left alone in the diningroom while Ayres spoke on the phone. It was then that he 'doctored' the bottle. Five minutes later he left the house, and Jacob Ayres was as good as dead.'

'But if Morris intended to kill why should he have suddenly made up his mind to run away from Dipton?' asked the Coroner. 'Had Mr. Ayres died on that night Henry Morris' action would have condemned him at once.'

'I said that Mr. Ayres was called to the telephone,' replied Blackmore. 'From the dining-room he could hear everything that was said, and Ayres was then asking his accountant to examine the books and draw up a partnership deed for his son. That news came to Morris one minute too late. He had already put the poison in the bottle. It had to remain there, and Morris left the house in a panic.'

'And rushed away to London,' said the coroner. 'Well, and what then, Mr. Blackmore?'

'I wish I knew,' replied the detective. 'We only know that he booked a seat in the 'plane for Paris on Thursday for Friday morning, but by then he had returned to Dipton. He did not have the five thousand pounds with him, for three of the notes were changed at Hurst Park race-course on the Friday afternoon, by which time Morris was dead!

'And he came back to Dipton, Mr. Coroner, risking arrest, for he must have known that Ayres was now aware of his colossal thefts,' Blackmore continued quickly. 'By footprints that are undoubtedly his we have found that he climbed the wall of Ayres' house some time during Friday afternoon. We have traced that at some time he hid in the toolshed, also we have found traces of his prints that prove he crouched in the shrubbery, from which place he had an excellent view of the study. It is possible that he was waiting to see, and warn Mr. Ayres, but that failed because it was there he was killed.'

'Are you able to prove that, Mr. Blackmore?' asked the interested coroner. 'I cannot allow you to bring chance guesswork into this court.'

'The sign of the struggles are there for anyone to see,' replied the detective. 'We have been able, also, to trace the dragging of the body deeper into the bushes, and from there are the deep heel-marks of two men who carried a burden to the wall. I think you can guess now how Morris was lifted over the wall and eventually brought to Turner's shed.'

As John Blackmore finished his story Jim Ayres jumped to his feet, but was immediately dragged down again by Jake Barnes. He sat there scowling viciously until the coroner had examined the rest of the witnesses, and the fury in his face deepened when a 'murder by some person or persons unknown' was recorded.

The court had no sooner broken up than Ayres was on his feet and making his way to Blackmore.

'You're just a sensational cheap-jack!' he said. 'You've dragged my father's name into this dirty business without any need. All this talk about Morris is just guesswork. You know the rat committed suicide, but that's too tame an ending for you!'

'In this country,' replied the detective quietly, 'we don't allow murder to pass unnoticed,' and turned his back on the man.

'It's murder and suicide!' bellowed Ayres. 'What good have you done Jacob Ayres by proving that he was murdered. 'You've shown that the man who killed him is dead. What more do you want?'

'The men who killed Morris,' said Blackmore slowly.

'My God! I think you are mad, Blackmore,' said Jake Barnes, who had followed his friend to Blackmore's side. 'It's plain enough that this fellow Morris got frightened, dashed for home when he found the London police after him, and committed suicide when he knew that Jim's father wanted to put him in prison.'

'He needn't have come back to Dipton to learn that, and he could have committed suicide in London just as easily as here,' said John Blackmore.

Jim Ayres' eyes narrowed.

'See here, Mr. Blackmore,' he said, 'lay off this game! There's nothing in it for you. You were asked to find Morris, well, he's found, and your job is done. Do you get that?'

'In my opinion the job has only just started,' replied Blackmore.

'Look here, Mr. Ayres,' broke in Inspector Moore. 'It's no use you making a fuss. We've still got to test Mr. Blackmore's theories. And if he's wrong I think he will be the first to admit it.'

'I certainly will!' declared the detective, with a quiet smile.

'That's not good enough for me,' said Ayres. 'What do I care about Morris? He robbed the old man for years, and he meant to kill him, or he wouldn't have studied poisons like he did.' He stepped closer to Blackmore. 'I tell you your job ended with the finding of Morris. If I find you spying round my house you'll get a taste of this.'

His clenched fist aimed at the detective, but Blackmore sidestepped him, and as Ayres lurched forward there came a click, as if two billiard balls had met in violent collision.

Jim Ayres' head jerked up and he pitched backward into the arms of his friend, but Barnes eased his fall and let him sag to the floor. Then he looked down at the man with an unfeeling grin.

'You asked for that,' he said quietly vicious. 'You fool! Now get up, and keep your mouth shut. Keep it shut, I tell you, or I'll shut it myself!' He turned to the detective. 'He's mad,' he said. 'He used to have these brainstorms in the East. Take no notice of him, Mr. Blackmore. I think he'll lift his hat next time he sees you!'

Blackmore nodded coldly.

'We are leaving Dipton in an hour, Inspector,' he said. 'If you'll come along to the hotel, I've got a few things to tell you that might be useful.'

7

The Stoker's Story

'You don't mean you're throwing up this affair?' asked Inspector Moore as they hurried out of the court.

'The Inspector's frightened Jim Ayres will think he's scared you away,' said Harry Cartwright.

The trouble in the court-room was already being whispered to the crowd who had left too early to see it, and many a stare was given the detective as he walked down the street.

'No, that wasn't the idea,' said the Inspector. 'But Mr. Blackmore has got all the threads in his hand and — '

'I haven't, Moore,' said the detective, as they turned into the hotel, 'but I've got a few. Here is Turner and Miss Reed. I think we had better go up to my room. Come along.'

They went upstairs and seated themselves round the table. Blackmore took an envelope from his pocket and shook from it a few scraps of paste-board.

'What do you make of those, Inspector?' he asked.

The Inspector peered at them.

'Looks to me like a torn visiting card,' he said. 'What have you done with it?'

'It's one of my own cards, treated for revealing prints,' said the detective. 'The first time I met Jim Ayres I noticed his thumb had a tiny white mark — the scar from a partly healed cut. I gave him my card with the intention of getting a print.'

'And it's not the only print with a wound mark on it that we've seen lately,' put in Cartwright.

The Inspector looked up, startled.

'The thumb-print on your windscreen?' he asked. 'You're not going to tell me that this is the same. It couldn't be. Ayres was still on his ship at that hour.'

'It is the same print,' Blackmore assured him. 'Either we've come across two prints that are exactly alike — and that is impossible — or Jim Ayres left his boat hours before we thought he did.'

'You're wrong there, Blackmore,' said

the Inspector. 'One of our men met him just as he was leaving the ship and gave him the news of his father's death. There's a mistake somewhere — you've got the prints mixed somehow.'

'That's why we're going to London,' said Blackmore. 'We must find out.'

'There's another thing I noticed,' said Cartwright. 'When Jim Ayres got mad, did you get the slip he made?'

'When he said that Morris had studied poisons?' he asked, and when the secretary nodded: 'I wondered if anyone else had noticed it.'

'But why shouldn't Ayres say that?' asked Turner. 'Mary told me of the book of poisons she found in Morris' room — '

'I don't think you told Ayres of that, Miss Reed?' he asked, and when she shook her head: 'No, I thought not, and the fact was never mentioned in court. I want to know more about Jim Ayres. I want to know everything there is to know about him. Do you remember him as a child, Moore?'

'Just about,' said the Inspector. 'He was only a nipper of sixteen then. He was a bad tempered young cuss, wild as they make them. He ran away from home.'

'He doesn't seem to have improved,' said Cartwright.

'No, but a man changes a lot in twenty years,' mused the detective.

'But not enough that you wouldn't know him again,' said the Inspector. 'No, he's Jim Ayres, all right. Besides, he's got a dozen letters from the old man, he showed them to me. And I know the bank have accepted his proof of identity.'

'And I'm sure he is Jim Ayres,' broke in Mary Reed unexpectedly. Besides seeing a photo he sent home five years ago, he spoke of my uncle, whom he used to know before he left Dipton. It was ouside the court this morning. He told me of the day when my uncle caught him stealing from his orchard, and he laughed at the chase old Tony gave him. Uncle has told me of the same tale many times. That proves he is Jim Ayres, doesn't it?'

'It seems to,' said Blackmore. 'Do you know how he is supposed to have spent the last twenty years — where, and what kind of job?'

'His father has spoken to me of him now and then,' said Inspector Moore. 'For some time Jim worked in Chicago, in the canning factories. He got into trouble there — I never heard the rights of it — then next time the old man heard he was in Alaska. He joined up with the Alaskan Mounted Police, and a rough lot they are, from all I hear.'

'Anything else you know, Moore?' asked the detective.

'A Manchester pal of mine went out to Alaska five years ago, and soon after he got there he mentioned Ayres in one of his letters. Said that he was hunting some fellow, and the betting was that Ayres wouldn't live the week out.'

Harry Cartwright had been listening intently to this conversation, and now he looked rather doubtfully at his employer.

'It's all very well knowing about Chicago and Alaska,' he said, 'but he's been East since, so they say, but there's somewhere else he's been, and for the life of me I can't think where.'

John Blackmore smiled and nodded.

'You've had your eyes on his right leg, my lad,' he said. 'You, too, have noticed that little slide that goes with each step.'

'That's it,' said the secretary, 'and it ought to tell me something.'

'Well, I've got the idea that that leg has been used to the strain of a weight.

The secretary's eyes opened wide.

'That's it,' he said. 'He's been in one of two prisons, that's how they label the dangerous criminals in Devil's Island and Sing-Sing!'

'Then you can rule Devil's Island out of it,' said the Inspector who was getting a little excited. 'It must have been Sing-Sing, for he'd never get out of the other place alive!'

'But he's supposed to have been East?' said the secretary.

Again the detective smiled at him, and the Inspector went on:

'When a man is returning to his family after being a long time away he tells his story for his own advantage. If he's had trouble in the West he won't talk about it, but tell the tale that suits him. Anyway, I can't see that it matters much where Jim

Ayres lodged during those years. Whatever sins he has committed I expect he's paid for, and now he has come home to about half a million of money and one of the finest mills in Lancashire.'

A look from Blackmore warned the secretary not to argue.

'Well, keep all that to yourself, Inspector,' he said casually. 'One other thing, Turner, it's about your weaving shed. I think the old man wanted to buy your shed, but Morris never meant him to.'

'No, because Morris wanted it for himself, Mr. Blackmore,' replied Dick Turner. 'I know what I've got there. I'm on a good thing, but it wants money to develop it properly.'

'That's just it,' Blackmore answered. 'Ayres had the money, and I can understand him wanting your patent. But Morris was in deep water. I don't quite see what he could have done with the business.'

'He could have sold it to one of the big syndicates,' said Turner.

'That might have brought him in a few

thousands,' said the detective, 'but he wanted a fortune, and he wanted it quickly to cover up his thefts from Ayres. Turner, I've an idea he was after more than your weaving shed.'

'I can't see what it is then,' said the young man. 'The old shed had been empty for years before I took it over. It's big enough for my needs, it allows me to manufacture enough to pay expenses, and I've the machinery there to complete my experiments.'

'Your foreman said the machinery had been damaged two or three times,' went on the detective. 'I'm wondering if that was to injure your business or for some other reason.'

'It was to make me sell out at scrap prices,' said Turner confidently. 'What else could it be for, Mr. Blackmore? The weaving machines were torn from their beds, dyeing vats upset, and boards ripped up all over the place.'

'Well, Turner, keep an eye on the place until we come back,' said Blackmore slowly. 'Morris wasn't working alone, and the people who killed him might want to carry on his work.'

An hour later they caught the express from Manchester, and on their arrival in London made their way immediately to Scotland Yard. To the record department Blackmore gave copies of the thumb-print he had made, but here they received a disappointment.

'I wouldn't like to swear that they were made by the same man.' said the record officer. 'They show the same flaw of an old wound, certainly, but in this one you haven't got a complete print. The missing piece might make all the difference, Mr. Blackmore.'

At that the detective left him and made his way to the office of Assistant Commissioner Brice, of the Alien Department, a shrewd man, with the dossiers of half the world's crooks on his books.

'I've never heard of Jim Ayres,' he said, 'and if he served a term in Sing-Sing I've no knowledge of it. 'I can ask New York about his service in the Alaskan Mounted, and I might tell you I'm interested in that bit about hunting that man. Five years ago, Blackmore, as near as I can remember, there was some trouble over that way with a crook by the name of Barton. 'Bishop' Barton they called him. He'd started life as a cub parson and turned rank bad. For years he practically ruled one part of Alaska. He ran a chain of illicit gaming rooms that were merely a cloak to other affairs.'

'I remember hearing of 'Bishop' Barton,' said the detective. 'Wasn't it the 'Bishop' who waylaid the miners who had struck it rich when they were bringing their gold to Dawson City?'

'That's the man,' said Brice. 'And more than one who dared to open his mouth about Barton was found dead soon afterwards. He was caught at last and his gang broken up. But they could never prove that Barton actually killed any of the men who had been found dead, and he got off with a life sentence — and that means to his last day, in America.'

'Well, I'd be obliged if you'll make enquiries about Ayres,' said the detective. 'I want to go along to that ship now, and from there, I think, back to Dipton. Perhaps if you know anything you'll write or phone me there.'

The Assistant Commissioner promised, and Blackmore left the big building, and made his way to the docks.

It was quite dark by the time he and his secretary reached the s.s. *Glonda*, berthed in the Albion Dock. Luckily the purser was still on board, and as soon as Blackmore stated his business, the purser's face creased into a smile.

'Jim Ayres — fine fellow,' he said. 'A hard case, though, Mr. Blackmore. You don't mean to tell me he's been getting into trouble already?'

John Blackmore hesitated.

'I don't know,' he said at last. 'I've an idea he wasn't on this boat when she docked, and — well, I'd better tell you what has happened.'

The purser listened in surprise to the strange tale, and when the detective had finished, he smiled.

'Well, you're on the wrong trail, Mr. Blackmore,' he said. 'I can tell you that Jim Ayres left the ship at one a.m. He was going to stay aboard until the morning, only some police fellow came along with news that his father had died, and Jim hurried off because he was wanted in the Midlands, I believe.'

Blackmore was disappointed, and showed it.

'That seems to knock the bottom out of my theory,' he admitted. 'Tell me, did Ayres ever speak of his life?'

'Many times, and many an interesting tale he told me. It was a long journey home, and we got very friendly during the weeks. He seems to have led a real man's life. He spent some time in a canning factory in Chicago, and five years in the Alaskan Mounted, where apparently he became known as 'hard hitting Ayres.'

'I heard something of that,' said Blackmore. 'I suppose he never told you why he left the force?'

'Yes, he did,' said the purser. 'Soon after he was promoted sergeant, he was sent out hunting a 'killer,' fellow called 'Bishop' Barton. According to Jim he was real hot stuff. Time and again he beat the police in his game of robbing, and it was always the gold diggers he went for. I remember Jim saying that Barton had an uncanny knack of finding out when one of them had a sackful, and as sure as nuts Barton would skin him, and Jim would arrive an hour too late. Anyway, it developed into an affair between Jim and Barton. Jim got two of his gang and he got three of Jim's. He got him in the end, though it was after Barton had made a clean-up in Alaska and retired on the proceeds in San Francisco. And it was the getting of Barton that made Jim chuck up his job.'

'When Barton got off with a life sentence, Jim said he had had enough. He deserved the chair ten times over if ever anyone did, but his lawyer put in a plea that nobody had ever seen Barton kill one of the men, and he got away with it. Jim said that that sort of justice didn't go down with him.'

'He had a friend named Barnes travelling with him, didn't he,' asked Blackmore, as they made their way on deck.

'He didn't, at least, not on this ship,' said the purser. 'Never heard him mention the name.'

They stood for a moment at the head of the companion-way.

'I'm sorry I can't help you any further, Mr. Blackmore,' said the purser. 'But you can take my word for it that Jim Ayres didn't leave this ship until well after midnight. When he did go it was with a Scotland Yard man, and they intended to hire a car to take Ayres home.'

John Blackmore nodded his thanks and walked slowly down the gangway, with his secretary behind him.

'Well, that's a dead end,' said Cartwright. 'I suppose the next thing is to try and trace Morris' movements from — What's the game?'

Cartwright jumped and turned quickly as cold fingers touched his neck, and he gasped with surprise to find a dark-skinned man at his elbow. The fellow must have followed them from the ship without making a sound.

'The purser all wrong,' he said quickly. 'Mr. Ayres do very funny thing. I know.'

Blackmore stared at him. In the pale light from the lamps the fellow looked a mixture of Slav and Chinese. And somehow the face seemed familiar.

'What funny thing did he do?' asked Cartwright before Blackmore could answer. 'Haven't I seen you before?'

'I am Lee,' said the man. 'Two — three years ago you saved me. A man was just to kill me with a knife and you hit on the head. I do not forget you.'

Like a flash Blackmore remembered.

'The Fan-tan club, in Lyons street! Did you come from the boat, Lee?'

'Yes, mister,' answered the man. 'Work on *Glonda*.'

'Well, if you've got anything to tell us we can't talk here,' said the detective sharply.

The detective hurried them along the dock road, keeping in the shadow of the wall. Cartwright was inwardly smiling as he remembered the incident at the Fan-tan club. Blackmore had actually caught a man trading a pound of cocaine to a Limehouse man. Somehow a rough house had developed and Lee had been in the mix-up. A hefty blow from his fist had saved the life of the man who called himself Lee.

In two minutes Blackmore had them in a quiet coffee-house and found them a table in a corner.

'Order something, Harry,' he said to his secretary. 'Now, Lee, if you have anything useful to tell us about Jim Ayres I can promise that you won't lose by it.'

'I don't know, but it look funny,' said Lee. 'I work in stoke-hole of *Glonda*. When we tie up boat I come up to get cool off. Mr. Ayres I see him on deck, looking up and down the quay. Everything dark and quiet.'

'Naturally, at that time of night,' said Blackmore. 'But go on, Lee.'

'Lee not supposed to be on deck, so I hide behind ventilator. I see two men come up the ladder and go to Jim Ayres. Not near to hear so go closer. Then hear one man say someone hurt coming to meet Ayres. He couldn't move, and they didn't think he could live day out. They say he ask for Jim, and was in street sounding like 'Dol' something. I not hear any more.'

'What happened then, Lee?' asked the detective.

'Mr. Ayres ran down ladder and went with two men,' answered this strange person. 'I stop on deck and think very hard. I just think not my job when I see one man come back, run up ladder and down alleyway.'

'What do you make of it?' asked Cartwright, as Lee's tale came to an end.

'That Jim Ayres has some queer friends,' said the detective. 'If Lee's tale is correct it means that Barnes or one of his friends came to say that someone — probably Ayres' father — was coming to meet him, and was attacked on the way to the ship. That they dare not move him and that he would not live long.'

'And that he was asking for Jim Ayres from some house in Dol — something street. Wherever can that be?'

Blackmore drew from his pocket a folded paper.

'There's a street map of London,' he said. 'Take the Limehouse district and look for the streets with DOL.'

Cartwright did as he was directed, and went through the district list muttering, Dolby, Doldobbin, Dolmere, Dolman —

109

'That'll do,' said the detective grimly. 'Chee Fu's den is in Dolman Street. It's not a very savoury place, but Chee Fu is too clever to be caught. I wouldn't mind betting that that is where they went.'

Lee's face had remained absolutely wooden, his eyes darting from one to the other. At the mention of Chee Fu's he nodded.

'Chee's sleep rooms. I know. I go when rich. I go Chee Fu's to-night if — ' and he looked meaningly at Blackmore.

'We all go to-night, Lee,' said the detective, and passed two notes to the man. 'If you help us you will get ten more, but if you give us away I'll have you put in the 'terrible house.''

The stoker shivered slightly. Like most of the Chinese and mixed races that worked on the boats he was not above trading 'dope' on his visits to London. He knew that the 'terrible house' meant a term in Dartmoor, and he had no wish to go there.

'I do what you want, mister,' he promised. 'I do lot for that money. Work hard, not get much.'

'The yellow heathen!' smiled Cartwright. 'But we can't go dressed like this.'

'Of course not,' answered his employer. 'We'll go back to Mecklinburg Square and find some suitable clothes. It's too early, anyway, to go there.'

The secretary took his meaning. At nine o'clock at night Chee Fu's place would be as quiet and orderly as a Sunday School meeting, but at midnight its grimy walls would hide more wickedness than the average prison.

8

The House of the Thousand Joys

It was striking twelve, and the Thames mist was thickening in the East India Dock Road, when three figures turned from the wide thoroughfare into the narrow confines of Ship Street. From there they turned and twisted in the narrowing network of alleys until they reached a short lane that appeared a trifle more ill-lit and grimy than any they had passed.

Dressed in creased cotton overalls they slithered along in single file, and on the extreme edge of the pavement, for all the world like coolies, and Blackmore and his secretary yellow-skinned and wiry haired, certainly looked the part.

Half-way down Blackmore stopped to speak to the other man, Lee, on whom they were dependent for their entrance into Chee Fu's.

'You know Chee Fu's place, Lee,' he said, 'and your job is to get us inside without raising suspicion. Once we are in your job is ended, you can do as you like. To-morrow I will see that you get the rest of the money. But should anything happen to us I've left word for the police to call on you at Chee Fu's or the ship.'

'Mister not fear,' said Lee cheerfully. 'You follow in behind. You all right. You friends of Lee.'

Turning into a pitch-black alley Lee knocked a double rat-tat on the back door. It opened an inch, and a circle of torchlight lit up his face. He was evidently recognised, for the door opened enough for his slim body to slip in, and the anxious 'friends' heard a sibilant whispering from the unseen guardian.

Then Lee's head popped round the door and he muttered a few words in his own particular dialect. But that was for the benefit of the doorkeeper, and he quickly broke into his stilted English without giving Blackmore a chance to reply.

'Come 'long in,' he invited. 'You got

dollars. Lee promise you spend them in Thousand Joys.'

The door opened wider, and Blackmore and Cartwright slipped in, to find the way blocked by a bull-necked Manchurian. He stared at them sleepily, but the visitors knew that behind the drooping eyelids keen eyes were weighing them up, and an alert brain was deciding if they were all Lee had said them to be.

A dozen different languages are spoken in China, so the Manchurian thought nothing of it when he spoke to Blackmore in his own tongue, and the supposed coast coolie answered him in guttural words that were strange to him.

'You welcome if you ran dollars, sailorman,' he said in English. 'Me keep door to see no harm come to honourable guests of joy shop. You find joy rooms along lobby.'

Blackmore guessed that the man was angling for a tip, so a shilling was slipped into the dirty paw. Then, with a brief nod he slouched after Lee without even a glance to see if his secretary was following.

And Lee appeared very much at home. Passing through a kitchen he trotted down a narrow passage that divided in its middle — a flight of stairs, very rickety, on one side and a closed door on the other.

The whole place was grimy and sordid. Filthy paper peeled from the walls, bare boards, hardly visible in the light of a single uncovered gas-jet. Lee gave his peculiar rat-tat on the door and when this was opened Cartwright had hard work to keep the surprise from his face when he followed Lee into the room.

Most likely the place would have looked ordinary enough in China, but here it was strange and unreal. An enormous room covered the whole ground floor. It was spread about with tables barely a foot high, brilliant cushions, and low divans in which men were sleeping. The hanging lamps were hidden by writhing snakes made of paper. The acrid bite of opium brought the tears to Cartwright's eyes, and he almost choked in an effort to keep from coughing.

In the centre of the room a wizened old Chinaman squatted at a table on which lay an uncovered oil-lamp, long, thin tweezers and a dozen tiny wooden pipes. Dotted about the room, at little tables, white, yellow and black men, played intricate games that were popular in China a thousand years ago. Sitting lazily in the shadow of a bronze Buddha was powerful Chee Fu, whom Blackmore knew as the uncrowned lord of London's Chinatown. He was drinking from a small glass, and his half-closed eyes were taking in every new-comer that entered the place.

'Drinks and cards upstairs,' whispered Lee. 'Make dream smoke for good of house, then after, just as home.'

So that was it. The wily Chee made it a rule for his guests to puff a little opium and after that they could do as they liked, and in their semi-doped state, wouldn't be particular how their cash melted, thought Cartwright.

The ancient at the table was already preparing pipes, and was certainly an artist at the game. Taking a tiny portion of the brown, fibrous stuff in the tweezers he quickly warmed it in the flame of the lamp, cleverly popped it, all aglow, in the little pipe-bowl, and added a red-hot cinder from a little brazier at his side.

Lee greedily grabbed the first pipe, took two or three long draws deep down into his lungs, sighed satisfaction, and then stretched himself full length on one of the divans. Cartwright's turn came next. He took one puff that made him feel as if he had swallowed a charcoal factory, and was glad enough to follow Lee to another couch. Taking a tip from Blackmore's action he kept the stuff alight by blowing through the pipe, keeping the poison from his lungs, yet even then feeling sick and dizzy.

But Chee Fu had no idea of putting his guests to sleep at this early stage. A dozen puffs and the pipe was empty — the victim dull enough to be rooked without raising a kick.

Chee had his eyes on them, and at the right moment sidled quickly over to Lee's couch.

'Dream smoke all gone, sailor-man,' he

said softly. 'Perhaps you wish make card game, or dlink?'

Never raising his voice he mentioned a dozen amusements to tempt his guests. But John Blackmore's almost closed eyes had spotted the table at which Chee had been drinking — the only table in the room raised to an ordinary height, its stained boards holding several clean glasses as if Chee expected special visitors.

'Make play — Fan-tan,' muttered Blackmore lazily. 'Get rich, go Shangai!'

'You play Fan-tan and get rich?' Chee whispered, his face expressionless. 'Yes, plenty dollar in Fan-tan. Make play this crowd.'

He looked enquiringly at Lee, and the *Glonda*'s stoker played up nobly.

'Him plenty dollars,' he muttered stupidly. 'Him good friends.'

He waved a hand at Blackmore and Cartwright, vouching for them in that half movement. Chee nodded briefly and led them to a table where a game was already in progress, and spoke in a whisper to a fellow at its head. The man was apparently one of his own men, there to gather any loose money that may be about.

Fortunately Blackmore and Cartwright had a good idea of the game — the past adventures in Chinatown had forced them to play it more than once. In this place they knew they hadn't a chance in a thousand of winning, but they cheerfully made ready to pay out 'dollars,' and keep their eyes and ears open.

At the next table two Limehouse Chinamen were whispering, their lisped words reaching even to the Fan-tan table in irritating snatches. In the quiet moments of the game they could hear every word, then a break, and they had to fill in the blanks as best they could.

''im say Mollis . . . said dying . . . '

Blackmore lost the rest of that, and the other man was speaking when he picked up the next words.

'Chee doped 'im . . . away in car . . . They not think I see, but Wu velly curious . . . think very strange . . . '

His words were drowned in a rattle of chips. Soon afterwards the pair moved away, but enough had been said to show Blackmore that his visit here had not been in vain.

A few minutes later that game was still on, and the detective was considerably lighter in pocket, when a man came into the room, a cloth cap pulled well over his eyes and a scarf almost muffling his chin. He made his way to Chee, and to Blackmore's surprise he saw that it was Jake Barnes, the man they had left in Dipton that morning.

'Fine mess you've been making of things,' he growled, as Chee handed him a drink.

'Nice hole you've landed us in. You better tell me what's happened.'

Chee nodded slowly and glanced round the room at his customers. Apparently satisfied that they were all engrossed in their gambling, he lifted a velvet curtain behind the Buddha and signed to Barnes to follow him.

Cartwright blinked and wondered for a moment if he had fallen asleep. The two men had disappeared so suddenly, it seemed as though the hideous idol had opened and swallowed them. Under cover of the jangle of chips Blackmore managed to whisper to his secretary.

'Room back of idol. Play on for a minute, then say you're cleaned out.'

They continued to play quite unmoved and eyed the dwindling chips with outward indifference. They lost quickly now and, soon the last few were thrown on the board and scooped away. Then Blackmore lazily began to stir.

'No play more,' he said. 'I smoke. Dream I win lot some day. You make pipe,' to Cartwright.

Cartwright nodded drowsily. Straightening up and ignoring the sly grin of the man who had rooked them, they slouched over to the opium table and paid for two more weeds.

'Quiet by honourable Buddha,' murmured the secretary, and made his way over to the wall near the idol.

Blackmore followed, and for a minute they squatted down against the wall, nodding drowsily. One or two glances were thrown their way, but they seemed quiet and stupid enough, and soon the players in the room had forgotten their very existence. Once Blackmore was sure they were engrossed in their games again, he began to edge nearer to the Buddha, his filmed eyes alert for the first suspicious move.

'Keep your distance,' he murmured. 'But when I'm hidden come quickly.'

Slipping behind the Buddha he lifted the curtain a few inches from the floor and peeped underneath. He could make out a narrow passage with a dim light at the end that puzzled him. Creeping into the lobby, with Cartwright close behind, he now saw that the light came from a cracked panel of a door, which luckily enabled them to see and hear into the room beyond. To their ears clearly came the voices, one was that of Chee, and the other belonged to Jake Barnes.

For some minutes they listened, hardly daring to breathe for fear they should miss any of the conversation that was going on between the friend of Jim Ayres and the wily Chinaman.

Suddenly a shrill voice came echoing down the passage, and the conversation stopped abruptly.

'You fella here — dollar all gone. You promise me plenty dollar if I get you in Chee's. Take all poor Lee's — '

Cartwright raced back and clapped a hand over the stoker's mouth.

'You damned fool!' he hissed. 'If I had you outside — '

But the damage was done. Chee Fu and Barnes moved to leave the room, and Blackmore had just one second to act. Snatching an automatic from his pocket he put the barrel to the crack in the panel and one shot plunged the room into darkness. A couple of bullets splintered the woodwork of the door, he had turned and was running along the narrow passage. Cartwright and Lee were at the side of the Buddha and the room was in an uproar — which was what he had hoped for.

'Police come! Douse 'im lights. Police coming through backway!'

Cartwright and Lee were on the edge of the crowd, and Blackmore's intention was to drive the panicky mob to the far door.

The secretary was still pushing and booting the bewildered and thoroughly frightened Lee across the room when Chee Fu and Barnes came from behind the Buddha, guns in their hands, and with murderous scowls that left no doubt of their intentions.

'Keep quiet, you dogs!' shouted the Chinaman, and Barnes was yelling: 'Where's that spy!'

At that moment the lights went out and the yells of the excited crowd were doubled.

'Put those lights up, you fools!' came the voice of Barnes.

'Policeman all round house!' shouted Blackmore, and for the sake of effect fired a couple of shots through the curtained window. The crash of the explosion, mingled with the splintering glass, nearly drove the half-doped crowd, frantic. In a surging, shrieking mass they packed and jammed in the narrow doorway — but by now Cartwright and his employer were well in the crush, with Lee squashed in between them.

Somewhere behind Chee Fu and

Barnes were shouting and imploring the crowd to quieten down. But the more they yelled the harder Blackmore and Cartwright pushed and heaved — their only chance of getting out unrecognised was to keep the men on the move. They burst through at last, staggered down the passage in the middle of the heaving mass, found the Manchurian guard had already made himself scarce, and raced into the open.

'Keep in the crowd,' whispered Blackmore to his secretary. 'They'll thin out at the end of the street and then we'll make a jump for it.'

'I don't like running away from skunks like that,' grumbled Cartwright. He heaved the panting Lee along none too gently. 'We've heard enough to know that Barnes is in it up to his neck where Morris is concerned, can't we try and rope him in now?'

'We could,' said the detective, 'but he would bring too many innocent people in it. We'll get him later.' They ran on. The crowd was now thinning to right and left, and nobody noticed the three figures that dived down an ill-lit alleyway. Cartwright thought they were lost, but to the detective this was familiar ground, and a still narrower entry took them through to the wide, deserted dock road. Here they were able to slow down.

'What are you going to do with this bright young thing?' asked Cartwright, glaring at Lee.

'For his own good,' said the detective, 'he's going in the police station. He was shouting his name all over the place, and you can bet Chee Fu heard him. No, Lee, you're going to stay in a comfortable cell until your ship sails again.'

'Lee no go prison,' wailed the man. 'Poor Lee do no harm — '

'What do you think you did there?' asked the secretary. 'If Chee Fu spots you he'll let daylight into you. Come on, you'll like a good British Prison much better than the stokehole of the *Glonda*, and there's not so much work.'

9

Bribery — and a Threat

'You know, boss,' said Cartwright at breakfast the next morning, 'the more I think of what that fool did last night the more I realise the mess he's got us into.'

'You mean shouting down the passage about us promising him dollars to get us into Chee's?'

'Yes,' said the secretary. 'He's given our game away.'

'Why?' asked the detective. 'If you remember rightly Lee didn't say *who* had promised him the money, or who was in the place with him. However much they may suspect they haven't any proof, and I can't see them getting any with Lee in the police station.'

'H'm!' said the young man.

'But they're going to make every effort to find out,' went on Blackmore. 'They don't know how long we were in the passage or how much we heard, but they will assume the worst. They will probably watch for Lee at the ship, and when they know he hasn't returned then they might turn their attention to us.'

'Well, they told us enough last night to prove that they are up to the neck in the killing of Ayres and Morris,' reasoned the secretary. 'According to what Barnes said last night Morris did kill the old man. That proves the theory you put forward at the inquest. And they've also shown that he was only being used by others. I think you've got enough to nail them on — '

'But I dare not use it,' answered the detective quietly. 'What did you make of Lee's tale of what happened on the *Glonda*?'

'I don't know exactly,' said the secretary. 'First he said two men came aboard the ship the moment she berthed and told a tale that took Jim Ayres away from the ship, and then he said one of them came back. Well, if I'm not the prize idiot! One of those fellows came back to take his place!'

Before Blackmore could answer the

surprise on the secretary's face was replaced by a frown.

'But Jim Ayres has been recognised in Dipton by several people,' he said. 'There was the tale he told Mary Reed about her uncle — that proves he really is Jim Ayres, without anything else, doesn't it?'

'It seems to,' said his employer, 'and we've got to get to the bottom of that mystery. But I'm certain that the Jim Ayres who went off the *Glonda* is not the same one who returned. Who is the real Jim Ayres, the first or the second?'

'Those two chinks who were next to us in Chee's,' said Cartwright. 'They were talking about someone being brought there, somebody being doped, and taken away in a car.'

'That will be the man whom Chee said he had placed in the hands of Dr. L. whoever he can be,' said the detective, remembering the conversation they had overheard through the broken panel of the door at Chee Fu's.

Cartwright whistled.

'Yes, I remember,' he said. 'Chee said that it was Dr. L. who gave the poison to

Morris. He said that the doctor would have his new guest as tame as the others in a week, and that after then he wouldn't recognise his home if he saw it.'

Blackmore's face was grave.

'There is a lot in this affair for us to find out yet,' he said. 'Doctor L., I should imagine, is a professional kidnapper, and an infernally clever poisoner.'

'I suppose that is why you won't clip the wings of Chee and Barnes. Even if you have these two arrested this other man is still at large?'

'Not only that,' he replied. 'The moment he gets suspicious he will make himself scarce. He has already earned the rope, and he knows that once he is caught nothing can save him. So you can be sure he won't leave any evidence about that can be used against him.'

'Then we've got to keep him quiet until we know who he is,' said Cartwright. 'And where he lives. Things are not very clear at Dipton. We've got to find out what Jim Ayres is doing with this poison gang, and we've still got to solve the mystery of Morris' attempts to damage

Turner's weaving shed. Seems to me that we've got a lot to do.'

John Blackmore had been standing a little back from the window, gazing idly out. Quite suddenly he stepped to the side and beckoned the secretary.

'We are having visitors,' he said. 'See who that is?'

Cartwright took one glance at the placid old Chinaman sauntering along on the opposite side. A benevolent old chap he looked, with tortoiseshell glasses perched on his nose — an amiable, harmless old Chinaman, so most people would have thought.

'Well, of all the nerve! Fancy Chee Fu coming here — after what we heard last night!'

'And how he laughed at us,' smiled the detective, for during the old man's conversation with Barnes he had dismissed Blackmore as of no account. 'I think it's because of what we heard last night that he's paying this call. He wants to find out if we know anything. He's a poisonous old snake!'

When Chee Fu sidled into the

consulting room at the maid's heels, he was bland and shy, and politely apologetic.

'You, please, are Mr. John Blackmore?' he asked.

'I am John Blackmore,' replied the detective, pulling forward a chair. 'Is there anything I can do for you?'

'Have bad trouble,' Chee sighed, shaking his head, and looking very sad. 'I am Chee Fu, keep quiet sailor-man's house in Dolman Street. You do not know it, Mr. Blackmore?'

That was a trap, for Chee must have known that John Blackmore was wise to the reputation he had with the police.

'Yes, I know it very well — the 'House of the Thousand Joys,' don't you call it?' answered Blackmore openly. 'You remember we went there once, Cartwright, after that dago who'd knifed his skipper on the — um — er — '

'The *Jose Ferando* — the fruit ship.' The secretary completed the sentence. 'I should just think I do. Though I didn't see much of the 'Thousand Joys.' He grinned as if the memory of the frousy den amused him.

'I am surprised that the owner of 'The Thousand Joys' should have come to me with his troubles,' said Blackmore quickly. 'I've heard of you, Chee Fu. You run a pretty tough place in Dolman Street. Who advised you to come to me, anyway?'

It was turning the tables with a vengeance, but Chee's face remained absolutely impassive. His bland eyes were as innocent as a child's, his answer as pat as if he had quite expected Blackmore to turn on him for coming there for advice.

'Me very, very sorry to bother you, Mr. Blackmore,' he lisped. 'But Chee Fu cannot go to police station. They not like Chee, not believe him, so Chee dare to come to honourable Mr. Blackmore.'

'Well, now you're here,' said Blackmore curtly, 'what do you want?'

'Bad man steal from Chee Fu last night. Steal valuable di'mond ring,' explained Chee Fu.

'Surely you don't expect me to find the fellow?' snapped Blackmore. 'You go to the police. You'll get justice from them the same as anyone else.'

'But Mr. Blackmore know the fellow quite well,' Chee droned on. 'The police not know him, but Mr. Blackmore do.'

'I know the man who stole your ring?' said the detective, genuinely amazed. 'What on earth do you mean? What's his name?'

'Lee. You know him, Mr. Blackmore,' Chee said softly, his head was bent and he was staring fixedly at the fireplace, but both the detective and his secretary knew that those slant eyes were watching their faces for the least tell-tale sign of surprise.

'Look here, Chee, don't be so confoundedly mysterious,' said Blackmore irritably. 'Is this Lee one of your servants? Why do you say I know him?'

'Him stoker on *Glonda*,' Chee murmured, as if that explained everything.

'Then why don't you go to his captain?' snapped the detective instantly. 'He's the man to complain to.'

'Lee not there now,' said Chee, unmoved by Blackmore's irritation. 'Chee been to *Glonda* already. They told Chee you there last night. Say you left with Lee.'

That was clever, and Blackmore realised the wily Chink might easily be
speaking the truth in this. He might have
visited the ship and have been told the
yarn of Lee stealing the ring — having
also made certain that the stoker was not
aboard. Also Lee might have been spotted
by someone stealing along the quay after
them.

'We were on the ship,' said the detective
truthfully, 'but we left it alone. 'Are you
trying to suggest that we hired Lee to
steal your ring? In any case, I can't help
you. I make it a rule never to take up
cases of petty thieving — '

'But Chee Fu willing to pay you well
— and it more healthy job than some you
do,' said Chee quietly. 'Chee very fond of
di'mond ring, he pay well. He pay — one
thousand pounds for honourable Mr.
Blackmore's help.'

Both the threat and the attempt at
bribery were plain, though Chee still
maintained his bland air of innocence.

'A generous fee, but I cannot accept it,'
answered Blackmore sharply. 'There are
two things I never do, Chee, keep out of a

job that is unhealthy, or take a fee I haven't earned.'

'Very sorry to hear that,' sighed the old man. 'Everyone know John Blackmore not afraid to die, but someday, perhaps — '

Chee Fu sighed and made slowly for the door, ignoring the cheerful good-bye Cartwright threw after him.

'Nice old man,' said the secretary. 'Willing to throw his money about if you'd stand off the Dipton case.'

'Yes, and a threat when I refused,' said Blackmore. 'He is not to be ignored, for we know already that to the poison gang life hasn't a very great value.'

'Except their own,' said the secretary.

'You'll have to stay in London, Harry, and watch Chee Fu,' said his employer. 'There are two distinct threads to this affair — Chee's dope den, and Morris' mysterious interest in Turner's weaving shed. Either might put us on the track of this Doctor L., the nicotine poisoner, so we'll have to split. I'll tackle the Dipton end and you look after Chee.'

'Right,' answered Cartwright cheerily.

'I'll get the run of the place by offering to find the lost ring — '

'You'll do nothing of the kind,' said Blackmore sharply. 'I don't want Chee to know you are even near the place. You must watch from outside and report any suspicions to me by phone.'

'If that's an order — ' said the secretary. 'It doesn't sound a bit exciting to me.'

Later he was to alter his opinion.

10

The Strange Story of 'Bishop' Barton

It was dark when John Blackmore reached Dipton, and after a quick call at the hotel he made straight for Turner's shed. Noise of machinery told him that work was still in progress. In the little office he found Dick Turner.

'Hello, Blackmore!' he greeted. 'Glad to see you back again. We're terribly busy.'

'Glad to hear it,' said the detective.

'If they'd only leave me alone,' said the young man, 'I'd be on my feet in twelve months.'

'They? Do you mean there has been more trouble?' asked Blackmore quickly.

Turner nodded.

'Somebody broke into the place last night,' he replied. 'Didn't do much harm, but two rolls of finished work had been moved, and by ill-luck dumped down by the dyeing vat and ruined. Now that

Morris is out of it, it beats me why — '

'We've got to find out why,' broke in the detective. 'Do you keep a night watchman?'

'Not in a little place like this. There's nothing here worth stealing. The weaving machines are no good to anybody, and everybody here knows that I haven't enough money to tempt a tramp.'

'It is evidently something worth others risking prison for,' was the reply. 'It seems strange that Morris should have bequeathed the ransacking of your shed to someone else. Is it possible to have a look round the place, Turner?'

'We finish in five minutes,' said Turner, glancing at his watch. 'But if you'd like to see the machines working we can go round now.'

The shed was not more than eighty feet in length, of a size that would make the average mill-owner smile. But Turner was already proving that he could deliver the goods, and his machines were never idle for want of orders.

'How long have you been here?' asked Blackmore, sniffing at the damp atmosphere, and noting the little pools of water that had gathered on the floor.

'Five months exactly,' replied the man. 'Of course, the shed isn't — '

'Never mind that,' said Blackmore, standing in the doorway between the office and the shed. 'I understand the building had been empty for years until you took it, is that right?'

'Yes, Mr. Blackmore,' admitted Dick. 'The shed was practically derelict when I came in. Windows broken, and the floor was so cracked that it was dangerous to walk over it.'

'Who did the place belong to when it was working, Turner?'

'Originally it was the beginning of the Ayres business. He started spinning here about forty years ago. That big place of his is the result of the money he made in here. During the war it was taken over as a packing shed for one of the hospitals.'

'H'm! You were talking about the cracked floor,' went on the detective. 'Is it usual to have a red-brick floor in a weaving shed?'

'No. It's want of cash in my case,' said Turner ruefully. 'It was easier to patch it up than put in new flooring. You can see where I've had new bricks put down.'

'That is what I'm looking at,' said the detective.

Just then the whistle blew, and he watched the workers pack up and depart with their cheery 'good nights' to the man who was more fellow workman than 'boss.' When they had gone John Blackmore beckoned Turner to follow him to the far end of the shed.

'There's a square here that has been entirely re-bricked,' he said. 'It is much larger than any of the others you've repaired. What stood here before?'

'The old Ayres mill had a cellar here for storing bales of cotton — it was really a picking shed under the old conditions. The cellar ran nearly the length of the building, but the trap-doors were here. When I took possession I had a lot of rubbish tipped down and the opening bricked over.'

'H'm! Then we're having some of the bricks removed to-night,' said the detective. 'But we're going to give those fellows that are worrying you a chance to come back first. And we're going to let the gossips of the town know there is something interesting in your old cellar.'

'But — Mr. Blackmore!' protested Turner. 'You'll have the whole population of Dipton thinking there is buried treasure in my shed, and there's been enough harm done already!'

'I hope that part of the population decides to come here once more,' said the detective. 'Anyway, Turner, I haven't had my dinner yet. You'd better come down to the hotel with me, and we can talk it over there.'

They talked for some time, but at the end of it Dick Turner was not much wiser than when they began. Blackmore was continually mentioning a certain IT — something that was hidden in the cellar and that they would dig into it on the following morning.

In the crowded smoke-room they found Jake Barnes, talking in whispers to a lean-faced man. At first sight of the detective Barnes frowned suspiciously, but Blackmore nodded brightly to him, and expressed the hope that Jim Ayres was not suffering any ill-effects from the blow he had received in the argument of the day before. They sat down at a table next to the two men, and Blackmore sat so that he was facing them.

'It is right enough, Turner,' he said loudly. 'Morris knew, and you've been rather dense not to have seen it long ago.'

'I suppose I have, Mr. Blackmore,' said Turner, playing up to the detective, but not knowing in the least what he was talking about. 'But how was I to tell — '

'By the fact that he had wrenched two of your big machines from the floor. Why, once he actually moved the big vat, didn't he,' said the detective sharply. He knew that curious glances were being turned their way, but he went on: 'It is obvious that Morris was trying to get through to the cellar. To-morrow, Turner, we are going to have the whole floor up — or at least enough for us to get into the cellar and make a search.'

'Well, if you think it is down there, Mr. Blackmore — '

'I'm certain of it,' replied the detective. 'But we can do nothing to-night. I've had a long day and need a good rest.'

'Very well,' said Turner. 'Then I'll see you at nine in the morning. Will that do?'

'Better make it eight,' said the detective. 'We'll have that flooring up before midday.' He finished his drink, got up and nodded shortly to Barnes.

In the hotel doorway, he shook hands with Turner and said good night, then telling the landlord to call him at seven in the morning he made his way upstairs — and then down again by the staff staircase, being careful that no one should spot him.

Five minutes later he joined Turner on the canal towing path that ran behind the weaving shed.

'Quietly, and don't show a light!' said the detective. 'We had better go straight through to the machine room. I think if we hide behind the engine we shall be all right.'

There was just room for them. As they settled down on the floor Blackmore noticed with satisfaction that the light of the moon illumined quite half the interior, the rest was in deep shadow, and when their eyes became attuned to the darkness they could make out the faint bulk of the machines.

'Mr. Blackmore,' whispered Turner, 'I know that you were speaking loud for effect in the hotel, but do you think the people who have been visiting me were there? Do you imagine that friend of Jim Ayres — Barnes — has anything to do with it?'

'I'm not sure,' said the detective. 'I'd rather keep an open mind. But I do know that he has had a big hand in the death of Morris.'

In low whispers he told Turner of the events of the night before, when they had gone to the house of 'Thousand Joys.' ending with the tale of the panic they had created to avoid being recognised by Barnes.

'Chee Fu called this morning to pump us, but I think he went back as wise as he came,' he said. 'I hope that Barnes doesn't think we were the cause of the riot. He can only guess, anyway.'

'Why not put Inspector Moore on to him?' asked Turner. 'You know enough to have him arrested.'

'I'm after somebody more important and dangerous than Jake Barnes,' said Blackmore. 'We can't put him away until we have got this mysterious Doctor L.'

'Queer looking fellow Barnes had with him to-night,' said Turner reflectively. He's stopping at Lynton Court — Ayres' place — I saw him arrive yesterday morning. Jim Ayres must be nearly a millionaire, now, and I can't understand what he is doing with a bunch of crooks — '

Turner broke off and looked at the detective. In the silence they had both heard a slight sound. It came from the office.

'There's someone in there,' said the detective. 'It sounds as though they were at your safe.'

'That's all right,' said Turner. 'There is less than three pounds in loose silver there, and I don't mind losing that to find out what the game is.'

They kept quite silent, and their strained hearing was as useful as if they were in the office. Two different voices came to their ears, both pitched so low that it was impossible to guess who they were.

There was the squeak of the safe door being opened, and several thuds told of Turner's books being tossed out. The bag of silver was flung down with an impatient exclamation. It was evidently not money they were after.

'He wasn't kidding!' said one voice. 'The packet must be down there still. We are wasting time here. Get the pick. We haven't got all the night to fool around in!'

For a few moments the two men stood hesitant in the doorway, and the watchers could see that they were masked and wore long, loose coats that completely hid their build. John Blackmore felt certain that neither of the men were Jim Ayres or Barnes, though he had a shrewd suspicion that the tallest of the two was the man who had been drinking with Barnes in the hotel.

'The Boss must have been daft to tell us to look in the safe!' grumbled the tall man. 'The packet must have been hidden here when Turner was a kid. I told you what Blackmore said, he was going to have the cellar uncovered to-morrow. Well, we're in before him, and we've got to find the old wooden trap.'

'I know something about these sheds,' said the second man. 'Used to work in one myself years ago. The cellar trap would be at the far end.'

They were quite close to Blackmore now, but they never glanced at the squat engine. With practised hands they made several strokes with the pick. Once the first bricks were dislodged they soon had a hole made and began tearing away at the rubble beneath.

And then the most unlucky chance brought about the discovery of the watchers. Dick Turner had been sitting in a cramped position, and in trying to ease his leg he touched the side of the engine, and something fell on the brick floor with a ting! It was a spanner that had been left on the low platform, and in the silence it sounded like a ton of metal.

The two masked men leaped out of the hole they were digging.

'We're caught! There's somebody here!' came from the shorter man. 'Let's get out!'

The tall man switched on a torch and threw the ray round the shed. Brightly it picked out the two men, and at the same instant that Turner jumped to his feet something hit him on the head, and he dropped. The detective knew he would have to fight for his life, and leaving Turner where he had fallen, got away from the machine. One of the men rushed at him with the pick, but he dodged out of his way, and the metal top of it hit the bricks.

'Drop that!' shouted the tall man. 'We've got him all right. Don't want to split him open!'

He made a rush at Blackmore, but his fist was ready, and it met the chin of the man with a click, that made him stagger. The second man apparently had no wish to fight on his own, and he made a rush for the door, pulling his half-dazed companion after him.

The detective turned to look for his fellow watcher and saw that Turner was just staggering to his feet.

'What happened?' he asked tenderly patting his head. 'Have they gone?'

'Yes, they've gone,' said the detective. 'There's no need to go after them.'

'I'm sorry you had to lose them through me,' said Turner apologetically. 'That swine must have thrown a brick at me.'

'Don't worry about the men,' said the detective. 'They've told me what I want to know. There is a packet hidden here, that probably holds the secret. We start where they left off.'

In spite of his sore head Turner smiled.

'They might have looked all night and never found it,' said the young man. 'One of them said the packet was hidden in the old wooden trap. Well, the trap isn't at that end. I used it to strengthen the floor beneath the dye vat. It's just under the bricks, here, Mr. Blackmore. I'm glad they left the pick. It won't take us long to get to it.'

★ ★ ★

It did not take them long to move the bricks, and in less than half an hour they had half the old wooden trap uncovered, and a little later managed to haul it out into the open. For a time they were puzzled to know how anything could be hidden there, but when Blackmore saw the dirt lines of a little slot in its side the mystery was solved.

'Someone has hollowed a drawer here,' he said. 'The wood is rotten. Pass me that pick.'

Three swinging blows splintered the wood right and left, and brought to light a stained and creased envelope, tied round with twine.

On it was an inscription in faded ink: 'The property of Henry Morris.'

'Well, this apparently is the reason why Morris wanted to get your shed. It must be important for him to have gone to all the trouble he did,' said the detective.

'He was away when I took over the place and made the alterations,' said Turner. 'But why couldn't he have asked me for it?'

'You were not on very good terms with

him,' said the detective. 'Maybe he thought you'd open the packet yourself. We had better look inside, and then perhaps we shall be able to understand.'

Carrying the stained envelope to the little office John Blackmore broke the rotten twine and took out a sheaf of papers. The first thing they saw was a picture of a girl in quaint old clothes.

There were several letters, too, and these told a sad story, one that uncovered a chapter in the lives of Ayres and Morris, and explained the reason for Morris' action.

Apparently Morris had a sister, Kate, who, against the wishes and advice of her brother, had gone to America with Ayres. She was soon disillusioned. Her lover was a bully and no saint, and would not marry her, telling her that one day he would be a big man and she would not fit into the position as his wife. He left her, and knowing the scandal the affair had caused when they left Dipton together, she hadn't the courage to come back. The last letter in the packet said that the writer would be dead by the time it reached

England, and that a son, Jim, three months old would be left.

Amongst the collection was a diary sheet and ran:

'My journey to Gilston was in vain. Kate is buried in the cemetery behind the town, but the boy is not there. Enquiries reveal that he was taken charge of by a person named Barton. They left here some time ago to try and make a living in the North. Have now one object in life — to make Jacob Ayres pay for his rottenness. This I will do.

'HENRY MORRIS.'

John Blackmore read aloud the note left by Morris.

'Well, according to the way he handled Ayres' affairs he seems to have carried out his threat, Turner,' he said.

'But he didn't prevent Ayres making a huge fortune,' said the young mill-owner. 'I can't see why he wanted to hide the papers if it was revenge he was after.'

'I can,' replied the detective. 'It's easy

to guess that when Morris returned from America Ayres had laid the foundation of his fortune. Morris could have talked, and caused a scandal that Ayres would have lived down in three months. He did better. He kept the old man under his thumb and bled him for forty years, no doubt constantly threatening him with exposure, and used Ayres' money to keep up a search for his nephew, Jim.'

'Funny that Ayres should have named his other son Jim as well,' said Turner.

'Morris must have found the boy,' said the detective, ignoring Turner's last remark. 'But by that time Jim was already ruined, and in prison.'

'But isn't that going a bit too far, Mr. Blackmore?' asked Turner. 'We've only just discovered the papers. We don't know anything about the child.'

'That note of Morris' says that the child was taken care of by a person named Barton,' Blackmore reminded him. 'I've no doubt that the boy was brought up to be a parson, too. But he turned bad, rank bad, as somebody remarked, and became the notorious

'Bishop' Barton.'

'Who was he?' asked Turner, and Blackmore told him what the Scotland Yard man had said about the Barton case.

'I believe those two were out for each other's blood, without knowing they were related,' said the detective. 'Anyway, Jim finally landed Barton in Sing-Sing. The rest of the story I got from Scotland Yard just before I came back to-night.'

Briefly he repeated the story told him by the *Glonda's* purser. Scotland Yard had enquired of New York concerning Barton, and had received in reply a coded cable stating that Barton escaped from prison a year ago. The affair had been kept quiet, for Barton was supposed to have been drowned when they were hunting for him the same night.

'There's no doubt that he got clear away,' finished the detective. 'And I suspect the whole job was engineered by someone in Morris' pay.'

'I don't quite see the connection,' said Turner.

'You will when I tell you that a warder was found dead in the corridor of Barton's cell,' answered Blackmore. 'There was no sign of injury on him. And it doesn't need much brain now to know that he died by an injection of nicotine, after what we've seen in Dipton.'

'Jim Ayres will be interested to hear that,' said Turner. 'From what you've told me this half-brother of his won't love him. Do you think we ought to warn him?'

John Blackmore shook his head.

'We don't know which Jim Ayres is here in Dipton,' he said. 'Think it over, Turner. The so-called 'Bishop' Barton is really an Ayres, and they are both hard cases. The 'Bishop' vanished a year ago, and Jim, the young, has been away from England for nearly twenty years. There was some queer work on the *Glonda* several nights ago, but was it that Jim Ayres heard that Barton was coming to England hunting him, and got the first blow in? Or was it that Barton was already in England, and that he laid a trap for his younger brother?'

Turner's eyes opened wide as he at last understood what Blackmore meant.

'What a position!' he gasped. 'There

are two Jim Ayres' in existence — these letters prove that — but they don't help us a bit to find if this man in Dipton is the real one! They have both lived in America for ages, and one of them has inherited more money than he'll ever be able to spend!'

'I'd like to see a copy of the old man's will,' said the detective.

'I can pretty well tell you what is in it,' said Turner. 'It was read over this morning. Except for a few minor bequests to the staff, he leaves the whole of his fortune to his son — Jim.'

'But which Jim?' said Blackmore.

'Don't know,' said Turner. 'I know the exact words are — "My son, Jim".'

'In law that means the one born in England,' said Blackmore slowly.

'And the one born in Gilston might be the one who has claimed it,' said the young man. 'It ought not to be difficult to find out.'

'Why?' asked Blackmore sharply. 'As far as the American police are concerned their man is dead — and they are not likely to believe otherwise. As far as we in

England are concerned, whatever we suspect doesn't matter a row of pins. The only thing that counts in an English law is cast-iron proof, and it is simply Jim Ayres' word against ours at present.'

'Do you think it is possible to get proof?' asked Turner.

'I think so,' said Blackmore quietly. 'You remember Miss Reed saying that her uncle knew Jim Ayres very well. Is the old man still alive. Does he live near?'

'He's alive,' said Turner, 'but he retired years ago. I think he lives in Southport. Mary can tell us that.'

'Then the sooner we get to him the better,' said the detective. 'If we get him here he might remember some peculiarity of the man, probably a birthmark, that will prove which Ayres we have in Dipton. But it will have to be done quietly, for I think the other one is in the hands of the nicotine gang.'

'Look here, Mr. Blackmore,' said Dick, after a pause. 'It isn't far to Mary's house. She will be in bed now, but I don't think she will mind seeing you if you tell her how important it is.'

'Not a bad idea,' said the detective. 'We will take these papers with us; they'll help Miss Reed understand the position and the importance of her uncle's evidence.'

Fifteen minutes later they were in the sitting-room of the Reed house, and Mary, still round-eyed with sleep, was listening with astonishment to John Blackmore's strange story.

'But Jim Ayres reminded me himself of Uncle Tony knowing him,' she said. 'It must be the Jim born here, or how would he have known of that little incident?'

'If he is the elder you can be sure he hasn't entered into this fraud lightly,' Blackmore answered. 'If he is Barton posing as Jim, how can we tell how much Morris has put him wise to? If it is a fraud it has been carefully prepared, and the incident you mentioned is just the sort of thing they would spring on you to convince you, and others, that this fellow is the real Jim Ayres. If he is, then we've still got to get his connection with the nicotine gang. Then again, if he is Barton, then the real Jim is in danger, and we've got to save him somehow.'

There was something so ominously serious in the detective's tone that his listeners shuddered.

'Your uncle may be able to help us more than any other person, Miss Reed,' said Blackmore. 'If we can bring him back to Dipton — '

'We can't do that, Mr. Blackmore,' said the girl. 'He is old, nearly eighty, and practically bedridden. He lives in Southport, and I'm afraid he'd never stand the journey.'

'Then can you go to him?' suggested the detective. 'You know what we want, any mark or scar he could recall would be enough.'

'I'll certainly go,' said Mary. 'But perhaps he mentioned something to my mother. If you will wait a minute I'll go and ask her.'

'Before you go, Miss Reed,' said the detective, 'are you on the phone?'

'No, Mr. Blackmore,' said the girl. 'But the exchange is only just up the road, and if it is important they will let you put a call through.'

'Have you thought of something?' asked Turner.

'I'm rather worried about my secretary,' said the detective. 'I left him to watch Chee Fu's place, and I wouldn't like him to come to any harm. While you see your mother I'll go along and phone through to Scotland Yard and ask them to get into touch with him.'

Mary Reed left the room and Blackmore went out to put the call through, little knowing then that he was too late!

11

Dr. Lumpert Visits Limehouse

In London the night turned wet and cold, but it was very suitable for the secretary's purpose. At dusk he made his way to Dolman Street. To have attempted a watch in his ordinary attire would, he knew, be asking for trouble.

Armed with a bundle of evening papers, dressed in a cap, muffler and suit that looked as if it had been slept in for a week, he had no fear of being recognised by any of the people who visited the house of Chee Fu.

He had a long and weary wait in the draughty doorways up and down the street. He saw many men slink into the alley beside Chee's den, but he was satisfied that they were the ordinary patrons of the place and of no interest to him.

It was cold, and there was not a light

shining in the house, every window was shuttered, and if it hadn't been for the figures creeping in one would have thought the place was empty.

From his shelter in a doorway Cartwright suddenly saw a car stop near Chee Fu's place, and in a second was across the road and opening the door.

'Paper, sir,' he whined, in true paper seller style. 'Late edition, mister?'

Cartwright's shrewd glance took the fellow in from head to foot, while he pushed a paper under his nose. The man was head and shoulders above him, and the light from the street lamp showed puffy lips and beady eyes glinting behind huge glasses.

'Clear off! No, wait a minute, I'll have a paper,' said the fellow quietly. 'You are out late. Surely you don't sell papers at this hour?'

The voice was thick and slightly guttural. Groping in his pocket for a copper the man moved slightly so that the lamplight fell full on the secretary's face. It was only for a second, for Cartwright was just as quick in dodging into the man's shadow again, but in that single instant the young man had the feeling that Chee's visitor had weighed him up and would remember him for days.

''Tis late, sir, but I often sell late this way — and sometimes sailors ain't above tippin' a fellow,' he hinted.

'Maybe, but I'm not a sailor,' was the reply, and he handed the secretary a penny.

He pocketed it and began to slouch off down the street. A cautious glance back told him that the visitor had slipped into Chee's place, and the chauffeur had settled down to a long wait. Cartwright edged back to his old position, a dark entry facing the dope den.

He had the feeling that his long wait had not been in vain, but had he been in the man's company for the next half-hour he would have been less satisfied, and probably have altered his tactics.

Once the door had closed behind him the midnight visitor made his way with rapidity. Nodding briefly to the Manchurian guard he raced upstairs to the first floor and crept quietly over to the shuttered window. Through the little round peepholes that were invisible from the street he kept a close watch on the entry opposite. When Chee Fu joined him some moments later there was a cold, vicious smile on his pouting lips.

'Very glad you come, Professor,' lisped Chee. 'Funny things happen last night — '

'We'll have that later,' whispered the man. 'I think your place is being watched. Keep your eye on that entry over the way.'

He had hardly finished speaking when the down-at-heel paper man slipped like a shadow into the dark opening. But the quick eyes looking down at him caught a flash of the papers he held, and when Chee watched through a pair of night glasses Cartwright could plainly be seen waiting inside the entry.

'I don't know what's been going on here, Chee,' said Professor Lumpert, 'but that fellow is sharp, and he's got his eye on this place. What have you been doing? I am beginning to think you have ceased to be useful, my friend.'

He spoke softly and without any appearance of temper, but Chee Fu's eyes filled with fear, and he stepped back slightly.

'You needn't be frightened of that — not yet,' said the other with a silky smile. 'Your phone message brought me rushing down here when I have my hands full at the home. I'm glad I came for it seems that I am wanted. Now you can tell me what happened last night, and if you wish to live, keep nothing back!'

In Limehouse Chee Fu was regarded as a hard man, but there was no question as to who was master now. It was quite humbly that Chee told of Barnes' visit and that panic that had so quickly sprung up.

Professor Lumpert listened quietly and without interruption; but the sneer on his face showed the contempt he felt for the yellow man.

'Sense, my friend, you have not,' said the man. 'When you found that John Blackmore and his secretary had visited the *Glonda* that settled the matter. That should have shown you who was spying here last night.'

'I thought so, too,' answered the

Chinaman. 'But to-day I go see Mr. Blackmore. Now not so sure.'

Professor Lumpert nodded.

'Your brains, I can see,' he sneered, 'are no match for John Blackmore. He has fooled you, Chee. Who do you think that is, hiding down in the street?'

'It is the secretary to Blackmore,' answered Chee, 'perhaps.'

'Perhaps!' said Lumpert. 'There's no perhaps about it! Never mind, he can wait until I am ready to deal with him. We must find out if Blackmore has returned to Dipton, if so, the others must be warned.'

'The machine for the wireless is ready,' said Chee, and he certainly did not look the placid old man he had done when he paid Blackmore the morning visit.

'That's good,' said the professor. 'We had better start to use it.'

They went up a flight of stairs to a big attic. This was fitted up with a complete transmission set. The whole affair would have done credit to the B.B.C.

For some minutes Lumpert fiddled with the knobs, and the hum of the dynamo filled the room, the note gradually lifting to a thin whine that told of the enormous power leashed and hidden in that slum dwelling. Chee Fu watched with interest while the professor tapped out a call sign — monotonously and patiently.

At last came the answering dot-dash-dot, the agreed signal that he was in touch with far away — Dipton!

★   ★   ★

For some minutes the man sat at the transmission board, and when he had finished his face was hard.

'Now, Chee Fu, you're getting out of here,' he said, in a tone that Chee would not have argued with. 'We are working on our biggest coup, and this place has become dangerous now that Blackmore knows of it. You'd better make that Manchurian dolt a present of the place.'

'And leave him to answer the police when they call, eh?' answered Chee cheerfully. 'You will play straight with me, Professor?'

Lumpert's eyes glinted.

'I am going to make your fortune, and pack you back to China,' said the man. 'But I need you to-night, and you must help me with our friend outside.'

Five minutes later Chee had collected his few valuables and had turned the house over to his delighted servant. On the step outside the trap was laid for Cartwright. Just a few words would do the trick.

'We must act now, while Blackmore is in Dipton,' said Lumpert in a voice loud enough to reach the secretary's ears. 'If they can keep him quiet for two days — that's all I need.'

He laughed softly and climbed into the car without a glance at the entry where Cartwright was hiding. Chee Fu followed, and as the car moved off they both looked out of the window the other side.

Dropping his bundle of papers Cartwright sprang noiselessly from his hiding place and vaulted lightly to the luggage rack at the back of the car. It made a good seat — he had room to sit sideways and wedge his feet against any sudden jolt, though after what he had heard he would have endured any discomfort.

At that hour the streets were empty of traffic and the car was able to keep up a steady speed. In half an hour they were clear of London and then the speed increased.

In the thin clothes Cartwright was wearing the cold seemed to go right through him, and he bunched himself up against the back of the car in an effort to keep warm. With the speed of the car and the wind it created as they flew along, it was impossible for the secretary to overhear any of the conversation, and he also missed the squeak of the back window as it was let down over his head.

The grind of tyres on the hard road told him that they were slowing down. He sat upright, prepared to jump down and run into the hedge at the slightest hint of discovery. Some sudden instinct made him look up. He saw the beady eyes of the professor staring down at him, and even as he realised the trap into which he had fallen, a crashing blow dropped on his head!

12

Chee is 'Paid Off'

The world rocked, and a million stars danced in front of Harry Cartwright's eyes. He remembered falling from the car and rolling over and over, but nothing more.

His first waking knowledge was of a fearful headache, and a jolting that seemed to jar every bone in his body. Gradually he understood that he was lying on the floor of the car, bound hand and foot, and that Lumpert and Chee were talking quietly over him.

'Whatever Blackmore guesses, what can he do?' he heard the professor say. 'His secretary has disappeared — he will ask many questions at your place, but your servant has no idea where you have gone. What is there to connect Dr. Lumpert's nursing home on the quiet coast of Yorkshire with an opium den in Limehouse?'

'John Blackmore very clever,' said the Chinaman. 'And this secretary, too, needs careful watching.'

'If he comes to his senses before we reach Millhaven I have something here that will keep him quiet,' said Lumpert. 'Once he is inside — well, let him try to escape. Nobody has done that yet.'

There was something so unnerving in the way the words were said that Cartwright instantly made up his mind to pretend to be unconscious — at least for a time. He had intended to bluff it out, demanding the reason for this treatment, but he knew now that it was useless to keep up the character of paperseller, and he bitterly called himself an idiot for falling into the trap.

When the car came to a standstill, nearly an hour later, Cartwright was feeling sick and ill, and it did not need any clever acting to play at being 'out.' He was dragged roughly from the car, and a bright light was flashed on his face; but his ghastly colour, and the great bruise on his forehead apparently satisfied the professor, for a curt order was given for him to be taken into the house.

Two men picked him up, and on the way he ventured a peep at the place he was entering. He had a glimpse of dark tree-covered grounds and a grey-stone house. A sniff of damp, salty air told him that he must be near the sea. Then he was dragged the length of a wide, well lit hall, and then laid on the carpet of a curiously furnished room.

The professor and Chee followed them into the room, and when Cartwright had been laid down Lumpert turned to the men.

'Loosen the dogs, Stern,' he said. 'And tell Mayes to take the guard on the turret.'

'Yes, sir,' said the man. 'The — guests have been very quiet since Milson tried to get away last week.'

'Andy Milson will run no more, eh?' asked the professor. 'You can lock up, Stern. I will attend to our new guest.'

'Who is he, sir?' asked Stern. 'He's not the type you usually bring here. He looks more like a tramp.'

He stood over Cartwright, looking down at him with an unpleasant sneer.

Through his almost closed eyes the secretary could see that he would be an ugly customer to deal with. The man was tall, heavy shouldered, deep chested, and with huge coarse hands that looked capable of felling an ox.

'I don't like curiosity,' said Lumpert, 'but this time I'll answer you. So that you will not be hoodwinked let me tell you that this 'tramp' is the secretary to John Blackmore, a man I respect more than all the dull witted police in England.'

'The devil!' gasped Stern. 'Wouldn't it be better to — er — put him to sleep, Professor?'

'No, you fool!' snapped Lumpert. 'You try that and you're finished. If Blackmore finds us, well, what can he do if he knows this young man's life is in danger? He is fond of him. We have three ways of escape, but none of them can we use if Blackmore knows our plans. At the worst, we can make him hold his hand; and at the best, this fellow can stay with the rest — when we have finished with him.'

Stern chuckled.

'He'll stay a long time,' he said. 'I'll be

in the strong room if you want me, Professor.'

As Stern softly closed the door the professor came over to Cartwright. In his hand he held a long, thin stiletto.

'How easy it is, Chee,' he said softly, 'to rid oneself of troublesome enemies. One quick touch with this — and the end.' The tip of the stiletto touched Cartwright's neck, but he never moved. 'But we have better ways in Millhaven, eh, Chee. Not even the knife is so swift or sure.'

'Professor Lumpert very clever man.' murmured Chee.

Lumpert grunted with satisfaction, he was not averse to a little flattery. With the knife he cut the ropes that bound Cartwright, picked him up with ease and pushed him into a soft easy chair.

'So, he still sleeps. We have ways of waking the nearly dead here. One touch of the needle and he will not sleep for days, eh, Chee? But he is coming-to now. He will be very surprised.'

Cartwright wakened slowly, and gratefully accepted the professor's tip. He stared stupidly round the room, and only after a time did he appear to notice the two men. He frowned, as if trying to remember, then struggled slowly to a sitting position, groaned, and placed two grimy hands to his throbbing head.

'Has somebody been using my head as a football!' he asked, and then: 'I say you fellows, what's the game. Where am I? Have I had an accident?'

'Yes, you have,' said the professor. 'And a serious one, too. You put your neck in a trap. Spy! The trap has shut — like that.' He slowly closed his fist until the white of the knuckles showed through the skin.

'What are you getting at?' asked the secretary. 'You let me out of this. I am going home!'

'Shut up!' shouted the professor. 'People who come to Millhaven go home — never! Look round this room. I want to show it to you so that you will not try to go home — until I let you.'

Cartwright had already looked, and wondered, but he made pretence now to be noticing it for the first time, and to be puzzled at what he saw. There was a surgical table, cases of glittering instruments, and in the corner a skeleton. Facing him stood a dentist's chair, with straps and grips that showed it was used for something more than drawing teeth.

'Is this a hospital?' asked Cartwright. 'Are you a doctor?'

'I will explain what Millhaven is,' said Lumpert coldly. 'In this room I make men and women different to what they have been before. I alter faces and minds. When I have finished my guests do not know their names, and their best friends would not recognise their features. Rich men and famous men have been in this room, and they left Millhaven as penniless tramps. Some of them have tried to escape, but they were afterwards found drowned far out at sea, or dead on the moors many miles from here. And their faces were changed so that none could even identify them.'

'Meaning,' said Cartwright, 'that if I try to escape I'm for it?'

Lumpert's face was close to his, so close that he could feel the warm breath of the man and see the glitter of madness in his eyes. He knew that he was in a particularly tight corner, but kept a grip on himself, reasoning that the more the professor lost his temper the more secrets he would tell, and perhaps in his boasting, drop hints that would be useful. With this thought in his head Cartwright set out deliberately to annoy him, but he had no thought of the awful sequel this was to have.

'I suppose you want me to promise not to escape?' said the secretary. 'Well, I'm not giving it, and I would not like to be in your shoes when John Blackmore gets busy.'

'Nor I in yours — if John Blackmore gets busy,' said Lumpert. 'You are safe just so long as he lets me alone, and not one moment longer.'

'You very silly secretary,' lisped Chee softly. 'Blackmore never find us. He is only in the way, professor.'

'I wouldn't be too sure, Chee,' said Cartwright. 'He knew I was coming to Dolman Street. And since you've left there doesn't it occur to you that he will hunt you to find me? Not only that, he's wise to your little game in Limehouse, and one word to Scotland Yard and by to-morrow the whole force will be itching to get their hands on you.'

He saw the fear leap into the Chinaman's eyes, and guessed the meaning of the glance he gave to Lumpert.

'It's all right for this Dutchman,' went on Cartwright. 'He's not being looked for yet. But every port will be closed to you, Chee, every chink in the country rounded up until they get hold of you. I haven't the least doubt that a dozen of your snakes saw you leave in Lumpert's company. How long do you think it will be before one of them squeals, and grabs the reward that is sure to be offered?'

'Stop that talk!' snapped the professor. 'You can laugh at him, Chee — '

'Can he?' said Cartwright. 'You know your own countrymen better than I do, Chee, but I'm certain they'd sell their own mothers for a pound. Lumpert's got you for a goat — '

'Is this true?' asked Chee of the professor suspiciously.

'You are a fool to listen to him!' said Lumpert.

'Perhaps I am, but perhaps he talk sense,' said Chee. 'He says I know my people. I do, and what he says is right.' He stepped between the evil-faced professor and Cartwright. 'Chee not want to spoil your amusement, professor, but think it better I get away before they start looking for me. You give me plenty money — '

'You are an idiot, Chee,' snapped Lumpert. 'Can't you see you are in the best hiding place already?'

'Until this young man is missed Chee can go where he likes,' answered the Chinaman shrewdly. 'So Chee go now. Get on boat for China then, cannot be found. You give me money, professor, then I can go.'

He spoke softly, but it was plain he meant to have his way. There was the tiniest flick of his loose sleeve, and a small automatic dropped into his hand as if by magic. He held it negligently at his hip, but its wicked black bore pointed straight at Lumpert's stomach, and the professor knew enough about fire-arms to have respect for them.

'Be reasonable, Chee,' he said coaxingly. 'You've allowed this fellow to upset you. See, he's laughing at you.'

'Chee know that trick, would rather look at professor now. Chee been a fool, now no more use to nicotine gang — '

'Shut up, you lunatic!' stormed the professor, slipping a pace nearer.

'Keep still, professor,' warned Chee. 'Limehouse shop no use to you now, so Chee see only one road to take. Please to give money, then Chee leave.'

'Put that gun away, and don't be a fool!' snapped Lumpert. 'Do you think I'd let you run loose about the country — '

'Chee not ask again,' warned the yellow man. 'You promise me car to go to London, then I can look after myself. Please, now, the dollars you owe me — my share of the business.'

The hand pointing the gun slowly lifted until it was breast high, and the gun pointed less than a foot away from Lumpert's heart.

'Easy, Chee,' protested Cartwright, for he could see that the Chinaman was in earnest.

'You be quiet,' said Chee, never taking his eyes off Lumpert.

'Oh, you'll have your money,' sneered the professor. 'But think again, Chee — '

'Chee thinking it easy to put me on the table and change face for me, like you said. Easy then to change brains. Now, or I fire you!'

'Don't! just say how much you want,' replied Lumpert quickly. 'You know I haven't much money on me — '

'Plenty in safe there,' interrupted Chee. 'Chee take ten thousand now. Call for rest some day.'

'Very kind of you,' said Lumpert. 'Well, I know better than to argue with a gun. I'll give you what I can.'

'Mr. Blackmore's secretary, you please will stand over there where I can see you,' said Chee to Cartwright, pointing with his gun to a corner, while Lumpert bent over the safe.

There was nothing else for it, and Cartwright took up his stand six feet from the pair. He watched them intently, for it seemed to him that the professor was playing with the Chinaman, though it was difficult to see what he could do, with a gun in his ribs.

'You're lucky, Chee,' said Lumpert. 'There's more in the safe than I thought.' In his hand he held a roll of bank-notes.

'Thank you,' said Chee. 'I take all of them.'

'I've no doubt you will,' sneered the professor, fumbling with the notes and finally holding them out with his fingers beneath the pile. 'Here you are, and much good — '

His insane laugh ran through the room, and to Cartwright's astonishment the notes fluttered from Chee's nerveless hand. The secretary caught a glimpse of something glittering between Lumpert's fingers, but his mind hardly registered the fact. His eyes fixed in wonder at that Chinaman, and he watched him sway like a huge pendulum. But he understood at last, when Chee crashed face forward to the carpet — dead!

13

Cartwright's Adventure

Lumpert bent to pick up the gun that had fallen from Chee's hand, but in that instant Cartwright saw a chance and took it. With a terrific leap he crashed into the professor and bowled him over the fallen Chinaman.

In a flash the secretary's fist closed over the gun and he sprang back, barely in time to escape the jab that Lumpert made at his leg.

'You swine!' he said softly. 'I can guess what is in that needle. Drop it, or I'll finish the work that Chee should have done. Drop it, Lumpert, you beast!'

His finger slowly tightened on the trigger, and there was something so ominous in his attitude that the professor flung the hypodermic needle at his feet. Cartwright was quick to sense the trap. He made no attempt to retrieve the thing, but ground it under his foot and stared at Lumpert.

'I wonder how many people you have killed that way?' he said bitterly.

The ropes that had bound him were close at hand, and these he kicked over without taking his eyes off the man.

'You're a rotten snake, Lumpert, and I'm taking no chances with you. Tie your feet with those ropes, and if you try to shout it will be the last sound you'll ever make.'

Lumpert looked up from the floor, but made no attempt to obey the secretary.

'You are as big a fool as this one,' he sneered, jerking his head at the dead Chee. 'You've got the upper hand of me now, but what good will it do you? You will never escape from this place — not if you had a dozen guns and men to help you.' He leaned upon one elbow and eyed Cartwright venomously. 'I have scores of helpers here. Do you think I'm fool enough not to have made escape impossible for anyone.'

'Don't know anything about that,' said the secretary. 'I'll attend to you first and find out about the others after. Come along, slip a noose round your long legs, then I'll look after your hands.'

'I'll not!' snapped Lumpert. 'You dare not fire. You'd bring everyone in the house down on you.'

'You're right, professor,' said Cartwright, and then, with a smile: 'Never mind, I think this will do as well.' Before Lumpert had realised his intention he had stooped and picked up the hypodermic instrument. 'The needle is smashed, but I imagine there is enough stuff left to keep you quiet.'

Without stopping to think whether he would have the courage to use it, knowing what it contained, he picked the thing up, and the fear in Lumpert's eyes told him the bluff was worth trying.

'Drop it!' whispered Lumpert in terror. 'You wouldn't use that?'

'Wouldn't I?' said the secretary. 'I'm not arguing with you. I've no regard for your life. Now, what is it, the rope or the needle?'

'You fiend!' snarled the professor, but he began to tie the rope round his feet.

'That's right,' said Cartwright smoothly. 'Pull it tight, Lumpert. Tighter! I'll have a look at it when you've finished. Now, flat on your back, and your arms above your head.'

In a flash he had passed a noose round the man's wrists, and in a couple of minutes Lumpert was well trussed and helpless.

Cartwright was taking no chances with him. There was work to be done, and in his shrewdness he guessed that on him depended the lives of other helpless prisoners. Once Lumpert was tied securely the secretary put an extra rope over his legs, then linked legs and arms together with a line round his back.

'You'll be a good man if you can get out of that,' he said. 'Now a pad for your teeth to chew on.'

'Listen to me first,' said Lumpert quietly. His voice was cold and bitter, the rage had dropped from him like a discarded coat. 'I am serious when I say that escape from Millhaven is impossible. In the grounds I have dogs, always hungry, ready to tear a man to pieces. In this quiet house there are a dozen men who know what the police will do to them if ever Millhaven is exposed, and that little gun you hold will never stop them from killing you.'

'Then if I had any sense I would kill you now,' answered Cartwright. 'What's the big idea, warning me of your own men?'

'To show you that you can do nothing on your own, and to make a deal with you,' Lumpert suggested slyly. 'Loosen me and you have my promise that I will let you go in four days.'

'That's a good tale, professor,' said Cartwright, trying to draw the man on.

'I mean it,' said Lumpert. 'Listen, I'll tell you a secret. I was clearing out of here in any case. Closing the business down for good. Once I'm away — I've a place to go to where I'll never be found, so it matters nothing to me then if you live. You can't get out of here, you'll only die in trying. You can upset my plans, you can kill me, but I know you won't do that, it is not the British way to kill a helpless prisoner.'

'Stow the sentiment,' snapped Cartwright. 'I'm making no agreements with you. I'm going to get out of here without your help, and I'm going to take those other poor devils with me.'

He'd had enough of the man's talk, and as he opened his mouth again he neatly slipped a wad of banknotes between his teeth. Over this he fastened a hand-kerchief, and when he saw Lumpert biting the paper he laughed.

'Those notes should choke you, Lumpert, if only for the way you trapped Chee with them. Now then, over with you. I think you'll just about fit under this couch, and you will be out of the way.'

With Lumpert disposed of Cartwright had to consider his next move carefully. He now knew for certain that he was in the headquarters of the nicotine poisoners, but as yet he had no idea as to why they kept up his tale of a nursing home, or why they had prisoners.

But Professor Lumpert was plainly the driving force and the leader of the gang. His boast of winding up the business in four days meant that he was bringing off a coup big enough to retire on, and he was not likely to leave any prisoners behind to give him away.

A glance at his watch told him that it was four a.m. It should be daylight soon, and there was much to be done. There was not a sound in the place and the eerie quietude was getting on his nerves. He switched off the lights and went to the window, gently pulling back the curtains that covered it.

To his ears came a shuffling sound on the turf below the window, though he could see nothing. There was a strong moon shining on this side of the house, and as his eyes grew accustomed to the changed light he realised that Lumpert had not been lying when he said there was no escape from the house.

On the smooth lawn he could see three huge dogs. Keeping them half starved, they were trained to be savage to any living creature that showed in the grounds from dusk till dawn, and Cartwright had a shrewd idea that others guarded every exit from the house. He could account for one or two with his gun, but it wouldn't be any use against a pack. The first thing was to find the prisoners, the dogs could wait.

With the gun poised and ready he crept out into the hall and listened with every nerve stretched. A light had been left, and a quick glance through the ground floor rooms showed him the ordinary furnishings of a country house. He might have been alone in the place for all the sound he heard, but the far off baying of a dog reminded him that Millhaven had its secrets.

Climbing cautiously up the wide, carpeted staircase, he was peeping down a long corridor when he became conscious of a droning hum above. It was broken now and then by a sharp metallic stab, and quite suddenly he guessed that an upper floor housed a wireless room, and that a message was being sent off in morse.

'If I can only get at that set for one minute!' he muttered. 'We are near the coast and a tapped message could be picked up by any boat or seaboard station.'

The corridor was in darkness, except for the moonlight that peeped in through two windows — two danger spots, if anyone was awake in the place. But the stairway to the upper floor lay at the end of the corridor, and the risk had to be taken if he was to reach that wireless set.

He had already crossed one moonlight patch when the very thing he feared happened. A door opened just beyond the second window, and he heard the slither of feet approaching on the polished boards. He had one glimpse of a thick-set man who was evidently on guard.

There was no chance of dodging, though at present Cartwright was momentarily sheltered by the deep shadows between the windows. He had just one second in which to think and act.

When the guard was within a yard of him Cartwright saw his eyes narrow and his hand creep to his hip. He was not certain of what was lurking in the shadow, and before he could free his gun Cartwright sprang — and hit!

His clubbed automatic hit the man squarely on the temple, and with a groan he pitched forward into the secretary's arms. Lowering him to the floor Cartwright first took away his gun, and then dragged him into the deep shadows further along the corridor.

By the noise the man was making he was not much hurt, and it was obvious that he would soon be waking, and in that case rouse the house. Cartwright's hands felt in the guard's pockets, hoping that in the capacity of warder he would have his keys. He was lucky, the keys were there.

His first idea was to find an empty room and lock the man in it, but he got the surprise of his life when he opened a door and a couple of men came blundering out.

The foremost aimed a swinging blow at his head, but he ducked and missed the blow. The glint of his revolver brought them up sharply.

'Put up your hands!' he whispered, 'and get back into that room! Don't shout. If I've got to shoot you're for it first!'

'But I say — '

'Don't say it!' snapped Cartwright. 'Here, pick up this pal of yours and take him into the room with you.'

'All right, but don't lock the door on us,' said one of these men. 'We've been trying to get through that door for days, and you're mad if you think this blighter you've put to sleep is a friend of ours.'

Cartwright realised his mistake and smiled. But he waited until the two men had dragged the guard into their bedroom and thrown him on the bed.

'If you'll tell me who are,' he said, 'perhaps I'll let you apologise for trying to bust my head.'

'Apologise? To one of that fiend's men? Not likely,' said the second man.

'I'm not one of Lumpert's men,' said Cartwright. 'But until you tell me who you are I've got nothing to say.'

'Then drop that gun, it looks nasty,' said the first man. 'My name is Herbert Seymour, I've been a prisoner here for three months. This man is a stranger to England. He came in three days ago. His name is Jim Ayres.'

'Did you say Ayres? Jim Ayres?' asked Cartwright in bewilderment. 'Did you come to England on the *Glonda?*'

A look of surprise flashed into the man's eyes.

'I did,' he said. 'And I haven't forgotten the reception I got. But what do you know about me, and what's the idea of being shoved in this hole?'

Before Cartwright could answer a deep groan from the bed turned their attention to the guard, and a glance showed that he was regaining his senses.

'Stuff something into his mouth,' said the secretary, 'and tie him up with these sheets. 'If he makes a noise now we are for it. I've just had a scene with Lumpert, and we are not very good friends.'

The two men were bursting with curiosity, but this was not the time to ask questions.

'I thought I heard a wireless on the next floor. Have you any idea where it is?'

'It's somewhere upstairs, but we've never been allowed up there,' said the man Seymour. 'We've been wanting a minute on that ourselves.'

'As soon as that man is tied we'll go up together,' said Cartwright. 'If I can get a few words out we may be able to get away from here.'

The man was safely tied, and as they left the room Jim Ayres asked Cartwright who he was.

'My name is Harry Cartwright,' said the young man. 'I'm secretary to John Blackmore, the — '

'John Blackmore! Holy smoke! I feel better already.'

But there was no time to listen to how Seymour felt, he hurried out into the corridor. The noise of the wireless could be heard, and there was no sign of another guard in the corridor. The two men followed him to the second staircase, which puzzled him slightly. It was of thin wrought iron and trembled with every step they took. But there was no time to think of anything but getting to the room above, though later he was to wish that he had examined the staircase more closely.

At the top of the staircase was a closed door, and here Cartwright paused and handed Jim Ayres the spare gun.

'There may be more than one man inside there,' he said. 'And we've got to get them away from the transmitter. 'If we can rush a single message through, then

Lumpert's poisoning gang is finished. Ready?'

Ayres nodded, and Cartwright flung the door open and jumped into the room. There was only one man there, and his head was bent over the morse key, phones clamped to his head. His back was to the door, but he was quickly aware that he had been disturbed, for the buzz of the machine stopped.

'Take your finger from that key!' shouted Cartwright, streaking across the big room 'And drop those phones. I want them!'

14

The Keg of Gunpowder

The man turned quickly, and seeing the gun pointed at his head gave in without a word. He was a pale and thin man, and the droop of his head and shoulders showed that he was no fighter, and when he dropped the phones and backed towards the door Cartwright hardly gave him another thought.

'Keep your eye on him, Ayres,' he cautioned.

Quickly adjusting the phones Cartwright twirled the tuner round to six hundred. His finger was pressing the buzzer and he was congratulating himself that another minute would see them through, when a streak of lightning seemed to flash from the set and every light in the room went out.

At the same instant a startled cry came from Jim Ayres, and two exploding guns mingled in one roar behind him.

'Stop him, Seymour,' he heard Ayres shout.

By now the secretary had dropped the phones, and as he stood in the darkness he heard the click of a lock. Instantly Ayres sent a bullet through the panels, but the clatter of boots on the iron stairway told them the shot had been wasted. And then came silence.

'Sorry, Cartwright,' said Ayres. 'He looked scared out of his life and I took my eyes off him just for a second to see what you were doing. He just touched a plug in the wall that busted the set, and I never thought for a minute he had a gun.'

'No more did I,' said Cartwright ruefully. 'He did it on us properly. Well, it's no use stopping here. The only thing we can do is to try and fight a way out. Come on! We'll have Lumpert and the whole gang at our heels in a minute.'

From below they heard a growing uproar, and any pretence at secrecy was useless now.

The locked door was shattered by a bullet from Cartwright's gun, the noise from the gun bringing an answering bark from the dogs in the grounds.

Tearing the broken framework of the door open the secretary was about to plunge down the iron stairway when some instinct prompted him to stop. It was well that he did so, for on striking a match he saw that the iron framework had gone, and only a great hole yawned at his feet. His toes were actually on the lip of the hole, and for a moment he turned dizzy at the thought of what he had escaped.

'That stairway was movable,' he said to the two men. 'They've taken it away, and we are trapped!'

'It only means a drop to the floor below,' said Seymour, 'Light another match. There must be some way out.'

Cartwright struck another match and held the flickering light so that it shone down the opening.

'I wouldn't take that drop, Seymour,' he said grimly. 'There's no floor below!'

The match flared and dimmed in eight seconds, but it was long enough to show the men a steel lined bore that seemed to drop for ever. The light lit up twenty feet of smooth metal wall, and Cartwright had a shrewd idea that the pit went deep down below the foundations of the house.

Groping in his pockets he found a few coppers. Leaning over the opening as far as he dared he dropped the coins straight down. It seemed an interminable time until a faint tinkle told him that they had struck bare stone, far out of sight, and almost out of hearing.

'This is Lumpert's trap against any intruders in the wireless room,' said the secretary. 'And probably a way of escape for the nicotine gang if ever the house is raided.'

He stepped slowly back into the room and saw with relief that dawn was just beginning to break. He could now make out the intricate machinery, looking ghostly in the half-light, and he grinned ruefully at his companions in misfortune.

'You've been longest in this place, Seymour,' he said. 'What do you know about it?'

'Not much,' Seymour admitted. 'I know it is somewhere on the coast of Yorkshire, and that's about all. One end of the grounds drops away to a rocky beach. I've been out under guard, and I've leaned over the wall several times.'

'H'm! then I'm right,' said Cartwright. 'That shaft is a way of escape. I'm certain that each floor will have a door opening into it, and I'd give something to know how they get down.'

'But there's no outlet — there can't be,' said Jim Ayres. 'The house is built a couple of hundred feet back from the cliffs. I've seen that from my bedroom window.'

'And I'll bet this shaft goes right down to the caves in the cliffs, and that Lumpert has arranged a get-away, if it comes to running,' said Cartwright. 'What bothers me is that I can't see any prospect of getting down to the caves ourselves. There doesn't seem to be a lift or a pulley here.'

A shrill whistle swirled through the room, a sound so unexpected that they jumped and stood ready for instant attack. It was Cartwright who first saw the speaking tube on the wall, and even as he pointed it out the sneering tones of

Lumpert filled the room.

'You're trapped, Cartwright, and as good as dead!' he jibed. 'It would have been wiser to have shot my wireless man at once.'

'I'd have been a jolly sight wiser if I had shot you!' answered the young man, with his mouth close to the tube. 'If the chance comes again — '

'It won't,' chuckled Lumpert. 'Let me see, you've got Seymour and our American friend with you. Well, they are no use to me any longer, so they may as well die with you!'

'We're not dead yet, Lumpert,' shouted Ayres. 'You've got us trapped in this room, but remember we are armed, and if you come within sight of us we'll shoot!'

'There will be nothing for you to shoot at, my friend,' replied the professor. 'I told you, Cartwright, that I was closing down my business this week. Your interference only means that I shall close down your part of it a little earlier.' He chuckled for a minute, and then his voice turned hard. 'It is light, do you see the hundreds of little holes in the ceiling?'

'What are they there for, Lumpert?' asked Seymour. 'Ventilators?'

'They are not ventilators,' said the voice of Lumpert. 'They are a little invention of my own. They are a spray — a vitriol spray!'

'Heavens! That's the game, is it?' Cartwright moved over to Seymour. 'Keep him talking,' he whispered. 'Try and get him on the raw. I've got an idea.'

His quick eyes had been studying the wireless fittings, and the sight of the indoor aerial had sent a fantastic scheme running through his brain. The wires zig-zagged up and down the ceiling, a spare coil was stored away in the corner, and altogether he judged there must be at least three hundred feet of silk-coated wire in the room with them.

While Seymour was annoying Lumpert Cartwright signed Ayres to help him, and they began quietly ripping the wires from their hold. Ayres was quick to take in the idea, and as fast as Cartwright released a length, he double knotted it at intervals of about six feet.

'So you've got a spray, a vitriol spray,

eh, Lumpert,' said Seymour light-heartedly. 'I like a joke myself, but I'll hand it to you. What's the idea?'

'To bring obstinate fools to their senses!' snapped back the professor. 'Once, before you came here, a mad Scotchman broke into my wireless room and killed the assistant. We got him before he could do any harm, but he had shown me the danger of another breaking into the place, and so I arranged a few little surprises. The sliding stairway — you fools should have guessed that when you stood on it.'

'We really should have done,' said Seymour, 'but we were keen to get at the wireless. But I'm interrupting you, Professor, do go on.'

The professor chuckled.

'And then I thought of the vitriol tanks,' he said. 'Over your heads there is a series of tanks, filled to the brim with vitriol! There is a lever at my side, here, and when I pull every corner of the room you stand in will be sprayed with liquid that will burn into your flesh. Your heads, eyes, hands, every part of you that it touches will be burnt. In two minutes you will be blind, in five raving maniacs, and in ten you will have thrown yourselves down the shaft to obtain relief.'

'Do you know, Professor,' said Seymour, with a smoothness that he was far from feeling, 'I'm beginning to think you intend to be nasty.' His eyes noted that Cartwright had the lines free and treble-reefed. 'I don't really believe in your vitriol spray. I think it is just a fairy tale that you have made up to amuse us. If you think you can get that staircase into position and rush us you've made a mistake, we've got our eyes in the passage, and the first nose that shows will be wiped out with a bullet.'

'I am wasting no time fighting you,' replied Lumpert. 'I am now going to start spraying. I will very much enjoy hearing you scream.'

Cartwright signalled to Seymour to try and hold him a little longer. He was fastening the three stranded wire to the powerful dynamo that was clamped securely to the floor.

'Half a minute,' said Seymour, 'don't

be in such a hurry, Professor. If this vitriol yarn is really true then we are not in love with it. Suppose we offer to give in, how will you treat us?'

There was a short pause. Pulling hard on the twisted wire Cartwright found that it held, and quickly lowered the hundred odd feet down the shaft. He beckoned Jim Ayres to go down first, but Ayres shook his head. Cartwright whispered that he must get off at once or the whole idea would be wasted. As Lumpert's voice came again through the tube Jim Ayres climbed awkwardly over the pit-head.

'I will not treat you at all,' said Lumpert. 'I have told you that you are no use to me.'

'But you've not going to torture us out that way?' said Seymour, cleverly assuming fear. 'We're willing to go back to your prison. What more do you want?'

Cartwright had been bending over the pit, steadying the wires and hoping they would take the strain. He did not want to add to the weight, but Lumpert could not be held off much longer, and the risk had to be taken. He took Seymour's place at the tube and motioned him to get going.

Seymour hesitated, made a sign for the secretary to go, but that young man settled the argument by continuing the conversation with Lumpert.

'Lumpert, you are beast enough for anything,' he said slowly. 'But there is one thing you are forgetting, and that is John Blackmore. There is nothing more certain on earth than that he will trace you and me through Chee Fu's Limehouse den. And if I'm not here when he arrives you'll be for it.'

'I will take that risk,' answered the professor. 'And I have finished arguing. But in your last moments I would have you know that by the time your stupid John Blackmore finds Millhaven it will have ceased to exist. I have my ways, and I can promise you that it will be many months before Blackmore will even find your bones! Now, watch the ceiling!'

But Cartwright didn't wait to watch. As Lumpert gave the order a score of thin streams shot down, criss-crossing, so that every foot was covered. The secretary had ducked and run, and a few splashes fell on his coat before he reached the edge of the pit and gently lowered himself over the edge. All this time he was screaming, and at the very last moment he yelled at his loudest, but once he began to descend he forgot about Lumpert.

He dare not hurry, for he knew the danger of chafed hands in such a position. In jerky little slides he descended, the knots in the wires staying his progress every few feet. Soon he was in pitch darkness, and was beginning to wonder if he would ever touch ground when his name was called in cautiously lowered tones.

'Keep it up, Cartwright,' came Seymour's voice, and before he could answer Ayres' voice called to him.

'They've discovered the trick! Get to the wall, man!'

Something whizzed past Cartwright's head. Another six inches and it would have brushed him from his hold. It was the table from the wireless room, but all it did was to crash to splinters somewhere below him.

The instant it crashed Seymour and Ayres were back at the bottom of the pit, holding and steadying the wire rope and encouraging the secretary. Other things were flung down. They heard Lumpert shouting in mad rage, and once a couple of shots were fired down the well.

Cartwright dropped the last ten feet, his tired hands could hold on no longer, but the two men were waiting for him, they caught him and hurried him from the shaft base in a second.

'Good lad,' said Ayres. 'Your brains saved us that time, Cartwright, but we're not out of the wood yet.'

Cartwright scrambled to his feet.

'I'd give anything for my torch,' he said. 'If only to see what kind of mess we've dropped into now.'

'There's one here, my lad,' said Seymour. 'I should think friend professor was prepared for a quick vanishing trick. There's food and all sorts of things down here.'

'We found the torch,' explained Ayres, 'but we dared not show the light while you were coming down. There will be no more argument. Lumpert will be out for blood now.'

'We've no idea how many ways he's got into these caves, either,' said Cartwright. He flashed the torch. 'My heavens, but they are some size!'

He was moving the torch slowly round and as the circle of light fell on the distant walls they stared in amazement. The place was roughly oval, two hundred feet in length, fifty at its widest and cut here and there by narrow tunnels. It sloped gently, arched to a huge dome overhead, and away off they could hear the lap of water.

'There's an opening to the sea,' said Cartwright cheerfully. 'That is our road, and we'd better make a break for it before Lumpert gets here.'

'We're ready,' said Ayres. 'I'll take the light and you two have your guns ready.'

They hurried on until they reached the narrowing of the cave. Beyond this they had to negotiate a zig-zagging tunnel fully a hundred feet from end to end. Their progress was very slow, for each sharp bend had to be carefully watched. Lumpert and his men were quiet enough, but that made it only the more dangerous.

They emerged at last into a smaller cave, but now they could see daylight and the glimmer of sea in the morning sunshine. The tide was almost at flood, the cave half full of water — a perfect secret harbour, on which a moored boat gently rocked.

But as their eyes took in this welcome sight a four-oared boat shot into the opening. There were six men in it, and one of them was Lumpert. He noticed the light a second before Seymour had time to put it out.

'There they are,' shouted the professor. 'Let them have it! Shoot them down!'

'Drop!' cried Cartwright, falling as the guns roared and echoed in the cave. 'We are too exposed here. Get back to the gully!'

It was only ten feet to the narrow cutting, fortunately, but bullets whined viciously over their heads, and Ayres felt a splinter of rock strike his cheek as they scrambled to a temporary safety.

'We are well in the soup!' said Cartwright. 'Lumpert is not taking us prisoners. He means to put us out! Well, it's not going all his way. Keep out of sight, Seymour. In this place our automatics are nearly as good as his rifles.'

'And we've about eight bullets between us,' said Ayres quietly. 'I've an idea we are none too well placed here. Lumpert is not holding back for nothing.'

'I was wondering that myself,' said Cartwright. 'But we've got time on our side.'

'That's just what we haven't,' broke in Ayres. 'What is to stop some of Lumpert's men coming down the shaft and taking us in the rear?'

'There's one of them coming this way,' said Cartwright. 'Look he's out of the boat. Can you see him hugging the wall?'

Ayres' answer was brief and to the point. He took careful aim, with one eye and the tip of the automatic peeping round the wall. He fired once, and before the echoing report had died away the man staggered to his feet with a shrill scream. He was gripping his left shoulder with his other hand, and for a few seconds he stood swaying blindly — if they had had the heart to hit him again he was a perfect mark. Then he sagged slowly to the ground, his knees bending as if the weight of his body was too much for him, then like a lame dog he began to crawl back to the boat.

'Let him go,' said Ayres. 'He's no use any longer, and there is no sense in wasting a good bullet. I'm going to have a look at the back.'

Ayres backed slowly, and Cartwright was left with his unarmed companion. Lumpert's crew made no further attempt to storm the gully, though every few seconds they chanced a shot in the hope of making a lucky hit.

'I hope nothing has happened to Ayres,' said Seymour, after a time.

'I think he is able to take care of himself,' said Cartwright.

'It's not so much that,' said Seymour, 'but I think he is right about Lumpert's men splitting into gangs. Look at those blighters out there. They know we're caged, and they are having a good laugh at us.'

At that moment Ayres crawled back.

'I've found a dug-out,' he whispered.

'Creep back along the gully and wait for me there. I'll give them a shot just before I join you, that will keep them quiet for a few seconds. Be careful of the loose stones.'

Seymour set off and Cartwright followed him, and just as they gained the end of the gully they heard Ayres' gun burst a single instant before a reverberating volley showed that Lumpert was warming up to an attack.

Cartwright was hesitating about going back to join Ayres when the latter raced into sight and passed them with a bound.

'They're landing, and going to rush us!' he yelled. 'Show that light for a second, Seymour.'

Helped by the light Ayres moved to the right, passed two narrow openings, and stopped by the third.

'In here! We shall have them all in front of us now, anyway,' he panted.

It was an ideal spot for defence, if only their few precious bullets lasted out. The hole was no more than three feet wide, less than six in height, and the scarred walls showed that it had been widened by man's handiwork.

'Funny place,' said Cartwright. 'I should think the caves are big enough for anything Lumpert wants. Why should he want to dig this place out of solid rock, I wonder?'

'It only goes back a dozen feet, and ends in a steel door that is double locked,' said Ayres. 'He must have something very precious in there. If we live through this we'll have the door open one day.'

But they had no time to think about locked doors in another second. There was a flash of light from the house-shaft, and they saw three more men come cautiously into view. At the same moment the men from the boat crowded the entrance of the gully, and each party started to send questions across the great cave.

'Have you seen them, Stern, they came this way?' asked one of the boat crew.

'We're looking for them now,' answered a voice. 'You're a mad lot to let them have the run of the caves.'

'That will do, Stern!' shouted Lumpert, pushing through the men and coming boldly into the middle of the cave. 'They can't have got away. They must be somewhere in the cuttings. Move those lights round, and keep them low, you fool!'

And that was the weakness of the place chosen by Ayres. A perfect stronghold for defence, it was not deep enough to hide them when the enemy lights began to pick out every inch of the walls. They crouched back, but very soon the lights crept nearer until one finally one pierced straight into the narrow opening and revealed them.

'Here they are, Professor!' cried Stern. 'They're trying to break into the strong room! If they get in there — '

'Shut up!' shouted Lumpert, and then jumped like a hare as a bullet from Ayres' gun flicked the tip of his left ear.

But he was no coward, and he emptied an automatic in the direction of the cutting — six bullets that were wasted only because the sloping floor protected the men now lying flat.

'Break up!' shouted Lumpert. 'Take it in turns to fire into that place.'

Signalling Stern and another man he began whispering to them, orders that sent them scurrying out of sight with horrible grins on their faces.

But the prisoners saw nothing of this, they were too busy trying to keep out of the way of the bullets and watching that their refuge was not suddenly attacked.

It was Cartwright who first noticed Lumpert's new move.

The whole series of caves sloped gently down to the sea level. When the secretary saw a small barrel rolling gently in their direction he didn't worry about it at first, but when he noticed that it was held by a double guide rope, and that whenever it went off the desired course the guide-rope pulled it back and again started it rolling to their refuge, he sat up and watched.

The next thing he saw was that Lumpert and his men had backed away to the far walls, and that they were, one by one, getting into the different cuttings. Those who remained kept up a steady fire in the recess in which the three crouched — and quite suddenly Cartwright realised what was happening.

'The brute!' he muttered. 'See that barrel, Ayres! I'll bet it is full of gunpowder and they are going to fire it off at us!'

Risking a belated bullet he stood boldly up and leaped to the mouth of the cutting. Holding his gun steadily he drew a bead on the keg, now less than thirty feet away, and fired!

15

John Blackmore Finds the Nursing Home

It had taken John Blackmore only five minutes to get through to Scotland Yard, and to Chief-Inspector Dikson he told the facts.

'I've left my secretary, Cartwright, to watch Chee Fu's place in Dolman Street,' he said. 'I'd like to know that he is all right. Will you find out for me?'

Dikson promised and said that he would call Blackmore back at the exchange in half an hour. The Superintendent was a very nice man, and allowed them to wait there for the return call.

When it came Blackmore's fears were realised.

A young man answering the description, of Cartwright, had been seen to jump on the luggage carrier of a car that had been waiting outside Chee's, and

Chee himself had been in the car with another stranger. Dikson was having Chee's place surrounded, and would call Blackmore again as soon as he had any news.

Less than fifteen minutes he was through again to Dipton, to report complete failure. Chee had given up the business and had gone away with the unknown man in the car, and the disguised Cartwright had left with them — on the luggage carrier.

'I'll do everything possible to trace him, Blackmore,' said the Chief Inspector. 'There are a dozen men hunting the district now. I've sent out an 'all stations' call to pull in any Chink driving out of London, and I've arrested every man in Chee's den, including that gib Manchurian. He says he is the owner.'

'Thanks, Dikson,' said the detective. 'It's important that I stay in Dipton, and I might get on Cartwright's track at this end. Phone me at the Dipton Hotel if you have any news.'

Dikson readily promised, and Blackmore replaced the receiver and turned to Turner.

'This has completely altered things,' he

explained. 'Ayres definitely knows that we are after him. Dikson says there is a transmission set in Chee Fu's place, and I wouldn't mind betting that that is the way they keep in communication with Dipton. And if they've got Cartwright they will get through to Ayres and tell him.'

'Let's go back to Mary's place,' said Turner. 'I said I would let her know what happened. She will be up and waiting.'

But a fresh surprise was in store for them when they arrived at the little house. It was old Mrs. Reed who answered the knock, and she stared in amazement at the visitors.

'I told Mary I'd come back,' said Turner, and then stopped as he saw the expression on the old lady's face. 'What's the matter? Mary is expecting us, isn't she?'

'She went out when she got your message, Dick, about fifteen minutes ago,' said Mrs. Reed.

'My message? What do you mean?' gasped Dick.

'You sent word Mr. Blackmore was waiting for her at the hotel,' replied Mrs.

Reed, and the fear crept into her eyes. 'She asked me to dress and wait until she came back — '

'But I didn't send a message!' interrupted Dick Turner. 'We haven't been near the hotel. I told her I would come back here.'

'Did you see the person who brought the message, Mrs. Reed?' asked Blackmore.

'Only from the bedroom window as they went off down the street,' answered the old lady. 'I hope there is nothing wrong.'

'Perhaps she is waiting at the hotel,' said Blackmore, to calm the mother's fears. 'Which way did they go?'

'To the right, towards the High Street and the hotel.'

'Then come on, Turner, the sooner we get to the hotel the better,' suggested Blackmore. 'Don't upset yourself, Mrs. Reed, Mary will soon be home.'

But away from the house Dick Turner could not control himself a moment longer.

'They've got her, Mr. Blackmore!

They've got her and Cartwright,' he said. 'But what could they want her for? What harm has she done?'

'The only reason I can think of,' said Blackmore, 'is that her uncle knows too much about the real Ayres. In Chee's place last night we heard Barnes say that Mary Reed would have to be watched. The fact that they've kidnapped her goes a long way to prove that the fellow posing here as Ayres is really the notorious 'Bishop' Barton. And that they should dare to get her in this way also proves that he knows his time in Dipton is short.'

'It doesn't matter to me what it proves!' said Turner. 'If they've got her they are going to know about it. I'll wring the brute's neck if he does her any harm. I'm going up to the house to have it out with him now!'

Blackmore tightened his hold on the man's arm.

'I'm going up there with you, Turner,' he said. 'But you will only play into his hands if you go up there making wild accusations. If they have kidnapped Mary you can be sure they haven't taken her to

224

Lynton Court, where a dozen servants would be ready to give them away.'

'Then what can we do?' asked Turner.

They had now reached the end of the street, and Blackmore paused before answering. At this point the main road turned towards the hotel, and almost opposite another lane ran out to open country.

'Whoever brought that message would take care not to let Miss Reed go near the hotel,' said the detective. 'They would not chance her meeting us. About here would be the place where they would make her turn away from the hotel, and if she made a struggle it must be almost at this spot.'

Flashing a torch-light on the ground he stepped off the pavement and stood examining the roadway thoughtfully. Quite suddenly he bent down and pointed to a patch of half dried mud in the gutter.

'There's been a car standing here, jammed right up against the kerb,' he said. 'And — '

Almost buried in the mud, he picked out a big button, grey coloured. It was one they instantly recognised.

'It's from the light coat Mary wears,' said Turner, in almost a groan. 'They've got her. Goodness only knows where she is now!'

'You can guess what happened,' said Blackmore. 'When those fellows dashed from your shed there must have been another on watch outside. They saw us go to Miss Reed's house, and they recognised the danger of her seeing her Uncle Tony.' He slipped the button in his waistcoat pocket and turned briskly towards the hotel. 'We'll get the car out and go up to Lynton Court, and see what is doing there.'

Shortly after they were outside the walled grounds of Lynton Court and driving slowly passed the locked gates. Turning the big car into a narrow lane Blackmore parked it under a huge tree where it was almost invisible.

To the two active men the eight foot wall presented little difficulty, and they were quickly creeping through the extensive grounds in the direction of the house. Approaching from the side they could see a room on the ground floor still lit up, though it was now long past midnight. Heavy curtains were drawn over the window, but they did not quite meet, and through the half inch peep-hole they were able to see quite half the interior.

The man they suspected of being 'Bishop' Barton was seated over a wireless set, another man had a pair of ear-phones clamped to his ears, and was sitting a few feet away. Even as Blackmore took in the scene he saw Ayres close down the set and turn with a laugh to his companion.

'We've got to get inside the house,' whispered Blackmore, drawing Turner back from the window. 'They are not awake at this hour for nothing, and it doesn't look as if Barnes is with them.'

'It's not difficult to guess where he is,' said Turner. 'Let's go! We can't get inside too soon for me.'

'Turner, if we have to tackle them not a word about Cartwright,' said the detective. 'The merest hint that we know he is missing will give the whole show away.'

The house was old, and Blackmore soon found a back window loose enough for his knife to prove useful. The click of the catch was the only sound he made, the raising of the lower frame was so gently done that not the slightest squeak came from it.

A flash of his torch showed that they were in the kitchen. Opening the door the detective stepped quietly into a passage, and almost immediately heard a murmur of voices somewhere ahead.

Guided by the sound he whispered to Turner to take a grip on his shoulder, and led the way with a hand touching the wall. Ten paces, then the passage turned sharply to the left, and a few more steps brought them to a door that was slightly ajar.

'It settles Blackmore, anyway,' Ayres was saying cheerfully. 'When he finds what Lumpert has done he is bound to rush back to London, and he'll be out of harm's way then.'

'You mean he'll be out of our way,' grunted the other man, and the voice was that of the man whom Blackmore had fisted in the weaving shed. 'I'm glad. He's got a punch like the kick of a mule. If I ever tackle him again it will be with a strip of lead!'

'There won't be any need to tackle him at all,' Ayres answered with a laugh. 'Lumpert has done the trick, you know what chance there is of getting out of his place. Blackmore will have his hands full without wasting time on us, and before he can return to Dipton we'll have skinned the place and got out.'

'But why can't you stop here, 'Bishop'?' asked the man. 'You're settled down as comfortably as any millionaire. Why not stick it and give us all a rake-off? There's enough for all of us! We'd be in clover for the rest of our lives.'

Outside the door Turner nudged Blackmore sharply. Here was clear admission with a vengeance, positive proof that the mill-owner was a fraud, and a desperate man whom the American prisons would be glad to welcome again.

They heard Barton yawn.

'Because it is too darned dangerous,' he said. 'I feel now as if I'm living on a volcano. A dozen little things can give the game away any second. Just imagine, any fellow who knew Jim Ayres in America has only to see my face and where am I? No, with that Blackmore fellow hanging around every chair I sit on feels as if it is an electric one.' He yawned again noisily. 'Wonder what's happened to Jake. He ought to have been here an hour ago. Told you he was only going to see Blackmore safely to bed, didn't he?'

'Sure! But you never know what Blackmore will be doing,' answered his companion. 'Anyway, we've got to wait up for Lumpert's O.K., so let's have another drink to keep the cold out.'

'No more to-night,' said Barton sharply. 'We might have to make a quick get-away, and I don't fancy a drunken man at the wheel. It's about time we called Doctor L. to see if there's anything doing yet.'

'He couldn't have got back,' said his friend. 'It's a good run from London to Yorkshire.'

'Maybe so. But Stern said he might be getting a message via London.'

The listeners in the passage waited anxiously, and it was only when they heard that Stern had not received any word from the chief that Blackmore took hold of Turner's arm and drew him away from the door.

Not a word was exchanged until they were back in the kitchen. Then Blackmore quickly explained his plans.

'We've got proof that this man is not the real Jim Ayres,' he said. 'But the moment we tell him so we most likely sign the death warrant for Cartwright, and probably several other people who are in the doctor's power.'

'You mean we've got to keep quiet and let him carry on his rotten game?' asked Turner.

John Blackmore nodded.

'Only until we find out Lumpert's secret retreat,' he answered. 'I've an idea we'll do that soon, and I think the stealing of Mary Reed is going to help us.'

'Good heavens! You don't think that Barnes is taking her to him?' gasped Turner.

Blackmore smiled grimly.

'I'm hoping so,' he replied. 'He hasn't returned to this house yet, and Barton's own words prove that they have no knowledge of her kidnapping. On the other hand Barnes will never think we made a second visit to her place. I bet he comes back to warn Barton of us finding the packet and his need for kidnapping Mary Reed.'

'It's driving me mad to think of her in that brute's hands!' said Turner.

'She won't be in Barnes' power for long,' Blackmore assured him. 'We had better get outside and watch for his return, then we're going to get busy.'

They climbed through the window and took shelter in the shrubbery where Morris had died a few days ago. They hadn't long to wait for within five minutes they heard hurrying footsteps on the gravel drive and saw Barnes tap on the study window.

'I suppose he dare not bring the car up for fear of waking the servants,' whispered the detective. 'They want no tell-tale tongues where the girl's disappearance is concerned. But the car won't be far away. Keep to the grass, Turner.'

John Blackmore's guess was right. A closed car stood just inside the gates with not a light showing. Creeping silently nearer they saw a man huddled in the driving seat, cap well pulled down and a cigarette between his lips.

He appeared to be half asleep, but when a twig snapped under the detective's boot he was off the car in a second.

'That you, Jake — ' he began. But the words died in his throat as something cold and round pressed heavily in the nape of his neck.

'Make a sound and I'll shoot!' whispered Blackmore. 'This way — out of sight of the house.'

'What's the game?' the man blustered. 'I'm taking the guv'nor up to London! If this is a hold-up — '

'It is!' answered the detective, pushing the man further from the drive.

'If you're car thieves — '

'We are,' agreed Blackmore. 'Now, drop that innocence! 'We want your cap and coat, and we want them without any fuss!'

'You're not damn well getting them!' said the man, trying to break away.

'You can go to prison for attempted kidnapping,' said Blackmore, 'or we can knock you on the head, take what we want, and have you arrested as one of the nicotine gang!'

'Who are you? What do you mean?' gasped the chauffeur.

'I'm John Blackmore,' said the detective. 'And you know very well what I mean. Now what is it going to be?'

But the man was already taking off his heavy driving coat and he submitted tamely when Turner appeared and started to tie him up with his own braces. They gagged him with a couple of handkerchiefs, and while they were doing so Turner whispered that Mary Reed was in the car — bound hand and foot and gagged.

'We'll put this fellow in my car first,' said the detective. 'It wouldn't be safe to leave him lying about. Then we'll see if Miss Reed will do something for us.'

The chauffeur was safely disposed of, and Turner was hidden in the driving coat and cap. There was still no sign of Barnes returning and the detective jumped into the car.

'Keep quiet, Miss Reed,' he said

slipping the gag from her mouth. 'We know what happened to you, and we've a good idea where they meant to take you.'

'Thank goodness you found me!' said the girl. 'He's been telling me of some horrible place in Yorkshire, a prison where no one ever gets out.'

'I want to go there,' said Blackmore, looking steadily at her. 'Cartwright is there, and our only way of finding this place is to let Barnes lead us there. Will you help by being brave and staying Barnes' prisoner for a few hours?'

Mary Reed smiled pluckily.

'If you think it is necessary, yes,' she replied. 'I'm frightened — horribly frightened! But I'll stick it out if you want me to, Mr. Blackmore.'

'Thank you,' said Blackmore, and patted her hands. 'You needn't be afraid of Barnes now. Turner is going to drive, and I won't be far away.' He jumped from the car and smiled encouragingly at the girl. 'You can have a word with Dick, and then we'd better put the gag on again.'

But he cut those few words short, for each moment he feared the return of

Barnes. Keeping a close watch in the direction of the house he tinkered about with the back of the car and gave a sigh of relief when his work was finished.

'Sorry, Miss Reed, but it's time to settle down again,' he said, replacing the gag. 'Come to the back, Turner, I've something to show you, and then I must fade out.' He bent down by the exhaust and pointed to something hidden well under the car. 'That's my pocket torch, and there's a full battery in it,' he said. 'The first chance you get switch the thing on — it is pointed downwards, and Barnes will never see it from inside the car. With this alight I can keep well back from you. I'll see the light half a mile away on a clear night like this.'

'That's great,' said Turner. 'If Barnes once had a suspicion that he was being followed he'd never go near Lumpert's place.'

'I'll hide in the bushes here to see that you get off all right,' said the detective. 'Then I'll get my car. Don't be afraid that you will out-distance me.'

'I'm not too sure of the road,' said

Turner doubtfully. 'I know the way to the Yorkshire moors.'

'It's night time, and if you go astray Barnes can't blame you. He will say things, but he's bound to give you the right road. You're job is to listen and say nothing!'

'I'd like to give him a taste of my fist,' said the young man.

But he looked harmless and sleepy enough when Barnes came swiftly down the drive a couple of minutes later.

'Let her go, Bill,' he called, jumping into the car with hardly a glance at the huddled figure in the driver's seat. 'Make for Ripley and Thirsk, they will be quiet at this hour.'

John Blackmore heard that and smiled at the valuable tip the man was giving away. The moment the car turned into the roadway the detective raced across the soft turf, scrambled over the wall, and eased his own car gently down the rutted side-lane.

He didn't hurry, for he knew that Turner would go easily until he was sure that Blackmore was behind him, after that he could be trusted to let her out and get the girl's ordeal over the quicker.

Blackmore had hardly troubled to keep Barnes' car in sight during the first hour of the run. He knew that his car could pick up the other when he wanted to. At Ripley he dropped his passenger, much to the amazement of the sleepy eyed sergeant-in-charge of the station, who only partly understood Blackmore's promise that the fellow would be charged later in the day.

It was not until Thirsk was passed that Turner stopped the car and emptied a can of petrol in the tank. From a couple of hundred yards behind, with all his lights out, Blackmore watched Barnes get out and stretch his legs, glance, at his watch, and snarl out an order for more speed. Turner nodded, pulled his cap a bit lower, and slipped round the back of the car.

It took him but a second to bend and switch on the torch, and Blackmore guessed that now the car would be driven at full speed. Seating himself comfortably at the wheel the detective gave Turner half a mile lead, then took up the chase.

Had he been less anxious he would have enjoyed the drive across Yorkshire. The drone of his high-powered engine quickly ascended to a whine, a satisfying sound that told him he was doing sixty.

There was no doubt about Turner's driving skill. Through little villages they took to the Yorkshire moors and soon reached a waste so lonely that it seemed as if man had never intruded there. The dawn was breaking, cold and grey, and something about the air told Blackmore that they were nearing the sea.

As the light grew clearer, he dropped further back from Turner. It was well he did so, for the first car suddenly swerved from the wide road and turned into a narrow rutted track. They were climbing all the time, a gradual incline that Blackmore now saw ended in an old wall and turreted castle, surrounded by extensive grounds.

This was undoubtedly Lumpert's retreat, and they were nearer to it than Blackmore ever intended Barnes to get. Like a swooping hawk he shot his car forward, it looked as if Turner's car had stopped, so swiftly did he overtake it.

And Turner was clever. The roar of Blackmore's engine warned him that Barnes was about to get the shock of his life. He swerved, and seemed about to crash into the wall that lined the road, and as Barnes' head came enquiringly from the opened window, he jammed the brake down hard.

'What's the matter, Bill?' yelled Barnes, 'Get her going — ' He jumped from the car. 'Who in Hell are you?'

At the same moment he saw the big car making for him, and realised the trap he had fallen into. His hand went like lightning to his hip, but before he could draw a gun Turner sprang at him.

The scrap was over before Blackmore could climb from his seat. The thought of the sufferings Mary Reed had endured for the past hours sent Turner fighting mad. His first smashing blow sent Barnes staggering, and the second knocked him moaning to the ground.

'All right, Turner,' said Blackmore 'No, you don't, Barnes, I'll have your gun!'

He tore the gun from Barnes' hand and sat on his chest.

'You'll find some handcuffs in my car, Turner,' he said. 'Bring them over.'

'You're a fool, Blackmore. You'll never get into that house, and I wouldn't give tuppence for your secretary's life now!' snarled Barnes hoarsely. 'You've been too smart this time. Lumpert will never let you take him.'

'We've got you,' said the detective, 'and we'll handle one thing at a time,' and he clicked the bracelets on his wrists. 'Take his bootlaces out and tie his ankles. That will hobble him. 'Into the car, Barnes. This is the end of your run.'

He waited while Turner gently lifted Mary Reed from the floor of the other car and cut the ropes that bound her. The girl nearly collapsed, and her cramped limbs gave her agony for a while. But she smiled pluckily, and never let a moan escape her.

'Well done, Miss Reed,' said the detective. 'We should have taken days to find this place without your help. You keep out of it now until we are through.'

'Having come so far, I'm going in with

you, Mr. Blackmore,' she answered. 'If they have wirelessed from Dipton that they have me in the car I'll be expected. I had better stay in the car or they will notice the fraud before you can get into the house.'

'You stay here, Mary!' said Turner. 'Great heavens, what's that?'

The surroundings were desolate, not a soul to be seen, but muffled and faint, as though some tremendous volcanic disturbance was taking place underground, came a dull rumbling! And Blackmore thought the roadway heaved beneath their feet.

His glance instinctively lifted to the old grey building, less than a mile away, and he stared in amazement. The others, drawn by his look of startled dismay, turned also, to see a huge corner tower break slowly away from the building, bend outwards, and crash to a heap of rubble.

'They've blown the place up!' gasped Turner. 'Look! There's another great corner falling!'

'And Harry Cartwright is somewhere

inside!' muttered the detective.

A laugh came from inside the car Turner had driven.

'I told you you'd been too clever, Blackmore,' said Barnes. 'If Lumpert is going out he's taking the others with him!'

16

The Madness of Professor Lumpert

'They're going to fire that gunpowder in our faces!'

Cartwright's shout brought Ayres and Seymour to the great cave on the run. They were in time to see the secretary point his gun at the keg that was now less than thirty feet away; but the sharp bark of his shot was lost in the roar that deafened them.

Where the keg had been a blinding flash of flame shot to the roof of the cave, and enormous masses of rock broke from above and on all sides. The flash was followed by suffocating darkness and the disturbance of air in that confined space whipped the puny humans like rocks on a storm-tossed sea!

'If that burst had been much nearer there wouldn't have been anything of us left!' muttered Cartwright stupidly.

He picked himself up from the rocky floor, slowly realised that no one had answered him, and began to feel about in the darkness.

'Hello, Ayres! Seymour, where are you?' he called softly. Then someone groaned close at hand and he heard his own name hoarsely whispered.

'That you, Cartwright — this way!' Ayres said. 'Seymour is hurt, daren't show a light. Those devils have got what they deserve. Listen to them!'

Now that Ayres had drawn his attention to it Cartwright could make out muttered groans all round him. Every now and then fresh sections of rock were dislodged from the roof, to crash down with terrifying detonations that meant instant death to any on whom they fell.

'The explosion has cracked the whole place to smithereens!' said Cartwright, crawling to Ayres side.

'You're right! It's tumbling about our ears,' said Ayres. 'But that little cutting must be near us. If we can get Seymour inside — '

'Here it is, just beside you,' said the

secretary, coughing with the reek of powder that bit into his throat. He found Seymour. 'Take his shoulders, Ayres. Where's the torch?'

As the pencil of light lit up Seymour's face they saw that a splinter of rock had cut into his right temple and that the blood was pouring from the wound. But when the light flashed on his closed eyes they opened slowly and he gazed round him dazedly.

'Earthquake hit me!' he mumbled, wiping the blood from his face with his bare hand and making an unsightly mess. 'Oh, I remember now. You blew the place up, didn't you?'

Through the heavy pall of smoke that hung about the place Cartwright could see tiny points of flickering light. As the smoke thinned and his eyes grew more accustomed to the blackness he saw that their hiding place was now sheltered by a great mass of shattered rock, for it was here that the main force of the blast had spent itself.

Ominous rumblings still came from overhead, and every now and then masses of stone smashed down and burst with the sound of thunder. It was a terrifying situation, and as Cartwright took in the whole eerie scene a huge segment crashed outward from the wall at his right, thousands of tons of stone that sent echoes battering to and fro as if a fresh explosion had taken place.

'The gunpowder must have broken the key-stone away,' said Cartwright, 'and the whole set of caves is collapsing. Looks as if it's going to carry on until there'll be a new map wanted for the coastline — and a new secretary wanted for the boss.'

'And the moment we move Lumpert's thugs make targets of us,' answered Ayres. 'How are you feeling, Seymour?'

'Like something the cat brought in,' said Seymour weakly. 'But I've still got eyes in my head. Look what's happened to the steel door behind us.'

Earlier on they had heard one of Lumpert's men say they were making for the strong room, and now they saw what he had meant. The steel door was bent and twisted until it stood drunkenly against the wall, and more than half open.

They were too dumbfounded to speak for a second or two.

'It looks like a treasure house!' said Cartwright in a whisper. 'Gold — in bars! All ready for a get-away in that motor-boat.

'Unlucky for us, though,' said Ayres, with hardly a glance at the fortune near them. 'Lumpert is not going to clear off without that, and we are in his way.'

'Look out! They're coming for it!' said Cartwright, from the mouth of the cave.

Fortunately Lumpert's men were forced to flash the torches they carried, for the whole ground plan of the caves had been altered by this terrible upheaval. Cartwright fired, and a scream told him that his bullet had found a home in someone's body. It was answered by a savage volley that sent lead spattering the walls about their ears, followed by a lightning rush that was meant to end the matter at once.

Stretched full length on the ground, Cartwright coolly emptied his gun into the dark mass, then flung the useless weapon at the crowd. Ayres took on the game. His first shot toppled a man almost on top of them, his second seemed to find an echo from the shaft that connected the caves with the house!

Before the harassed defenders really guessed that help was at hand, a staccato outburst of drum firing mingled with the startled yells of Lumpert's survivors.

'Make for the boat. It's our only way!' called the man Stern.

'Attack the shaft!' came from Lumpert in the darkness. 'There's only two — ' The hoarse yell suddenly lifted to a frenzied scream and snapped off short. That was enough for the bewildered crowd, and the fusillade from the shaft drove them in a panicky rush through the passage to the sea.

'Cartwright! Cartwright! Where are you?' came the call.

'Mr. Blackmore! How on earth did you get here?' shouted Cartwright, and in his haste to get out fell headlong into a pile of rock. 'They're getting away, but I think Lumpert is down.'

'Come on, Turner,' called Blackmore to the shadowy figure behind him. 'We want Lumpert most, but we must try and stop those fellows getting word through to Dipton.'

But they found it impossible to hurry through those dangerous passages. The whole place was cracking and breaking. They had to creep along by the walls, and several times to make wild detours to avoid huge overhanging slabs that were ready to fall with a touch.

'You three men look out for Lumpert,' said Blackmore quickly. 'We'll try and get through to the sea. Do you know the way, Cartwright?'

'If it is still open,' said his secretary doubtfully. 'Here is the passage. Hell! It's in ruins!'

As John Blackmore pointed his torch down the narrow way they saw the figure of a man just topping a great heap of stone that had crashed from the roof. As the light fell on him he turned his face to them, and they saw it was the wounded professor.

A bullet had ploughed a furrow from chin to ear, and blood was gushing from the wound in his shoulder. The disastrous events of the last hour had turned him into a dangerous lunatic. His glittering eyes and bared teeth showed that he was capable of any outrage, and when Blackmore called to him to stop he scrambled awkwardly to his feet and stood swaying unsteadily on the heap.

'You've got me, Blackmore. I knew you'd turn up one day. I had a reception for you, but your secretary upset it. But you're not out yet! I've still got something for you — it's this!'

Blackmore fired, but Lumpert jumped out of sight a second before. From the far side of the mound they heard his insane laugh, then a small metal object came whirling back, hit the low roof, and burst!

The alert detective sent Cartwright flying back with a push in the chest, and threw himself flat. The flash of a bursting bomb was followed by a terrific shattering of stone. Already weakened and cracked in a score of places, the walls and roof simply caved in, and the exit to the sea vanished for ever!

'He'd made preparations for you all right,' groaned Cartwright, sitting up and rubbing his head where a flying fragment had touched him. 'I hope we've come to the end of them. I've had about enough of the professor's prize packets.'

'If he gets back to the house before us we'll have the biggest surprise of them all,' snapped Blackmore. 'Another bomb down that shaft and we'll be taking permanent lodgings in these caves.'

The mere thought of such a fate sent Cartwright to the great cave on the run. The others were coming to meet them, and the sight of the uninjured pair brought relief to their faces.

'This is the real Jim Ayres,' said the secretary, as they met. 'And this is Herbert Seymour. They have both been prisoners of Lumpert's.'

'There's five of the gang here, Mr. Blackmore,' said Ayres quickly. 'Three-dead, and two badly wounded. We can't leave — '

'You look after them,' said the detective. 'Lumpert is dangerous, and we've left a girl above — '

Dick Turner gave an oath and ran from them. Fortunately they had no need to use the wire rope by which Cartwright and the others had descended the pit — a small open lift was Lumpert's line of communication to the house from the cave.

There was just room for Blackmore, Cartwright and Turner. The electric power had been snapped in the explosion, but the double ropes by which it worked allowed them to pull it up to ground level in a couple of minutes.

As they stepped through the sliding panel to the lower floor, of Millhaven, Cartwright was astonished to find the house almost in ruins. Cracked and broken walls, shattered glass, and a huge gaping hole where Lumpert's operating room had stood now met his gaze, and distant rumblings told him that even yet the old grey walls were tumbling in some part of the building.

'It's a marvel that the shaft stood firm!' he said.

'Only because it was lined with steel,' said the detective. 'But I'm anxious about Miss Reed. Let's hurry, Turner.'

Because of the danger of falling masonry they had been forced to leave the two cars a couple of hundred yards from the house. As they rushed to the open Blackmore gave a shout and raced across the uneven turf. A moment later Turner and Cartwright came through the twisted doorway and saw the cause of the panic speed. Lumpert running down the rutted road from the cliffs, and now less than thirty feet away from the two cars.

Until Blackmore shot from the house the cunning professor had been creeping silently towards the cars, his eyes fixed on the unsuspecting girl that guarded them. Her head was nodding, for the strain of the sleepless night had tired her, but Blackmore's shout roused her to a sense of her danger.

She sprang from the car in a second, but before she had gone three uncertain steps Lumpert was on her. With ease he lifted her from the ground and with a horrible grin on his torn face he bounded to the car in which Jake Barnes was lying a prisoner. Pushing the girl to the seat he jumped in behind the wheel, threw in the clutch, turned the car from the road to the smooth turf, and went speeding up the hill.

John Blackmore never once looked back to see if Cartwright or Turner had followed him. His face was white and set, for he was sure that Lumpert was a raving madman, and for the moment he thought the fellow was going to drive the car over the cliffs and plunge to certain death on the rocks below.

But nothing was further from Lumpert's thoughts. As Blackmore dropped into the driving seat of his own car the one in front swerved inland and vanished over a hillock. Turner and the secretary just managed to grip the sides of the car and as Blackmore shot away they tumbled into the back.

The first ten seconds nearly brought disaster. A cunning trap that proved that Lumpert's twisted mind still reasoned coherently. As Blackmore's car gained the hill-top the three startled pursuers saw a terrifying drop fronting them — a steep incline covered with furze bush, and a nightmare descent at the speed they were now going.

Lumpert's car was now creeping down like a crab — twisting and turning to avoid huge boulders, and never once showing a straight front to the drop. The detective had shot down a good thirty yards before he had the car under control. But an instant's hesitation would have meant a head on crash and broken necks. For a few seconds the car twisted like a snake, but Blackmore managed to ease her to a standstill.

It was only now that Lumpert's clever move was fully revealed. Cartwright's first anxious glance showed him that the doctor's car had turned again the moment they shot over the rise. Lumpert was going back on his tracks and they were a hundred yards downhill!

'The swine!' shouted Turner. 'He's making for the road again, and he cut himself out a good lead.'

In spite of all he had suffered at the poisoner's hands Cartwright felt a moment's admiration for the fellow's cunning. But Dick Turner had only one thought in his head the terrible danger to the girl who meant everything to him.

'Great heavens, Blackmore?' he groaned. 'Isn't there any way of saving her?'

For answer Blackmore started the car

and turned it in a wide sweep.

'He'll hold on to her till the last second.'

Turner sank back with a groan. To his tortured mind it looked as if Mary was doomed in any case. But John Blackmore's lips were set in grim lines, for he was remembering that he had persuaded the girl to act as decoy for them and that she owed her terrible plight to playing his game.

'Buck up,' whispered Cartwright to Turner, as Blackmore forced the car carefully up-hill. 'Once we get on the road no car has a chance with this one. And I've got an idea for when we get near. We're not beaten yet.' He stood up as the car topped the rise at last. 'There she goes — two miles lead and heading straight for the moors!'

There was hardly another word spoken during the long chase that followed. Crouched over the wheel Blackmore's skilful hands brought astonishing speed from the car.

A howling gale roared past, and every tiny pebble they touched sent a throb through the car as if a hammer had struck it. Lumpert was giving them a good run. The car was capable of more speed than Blackmore had reckoned.

They had no idea in which direction the professor was making, they doubted if he had any definite plan in mind at all, bar escape. But they were closing with him now, and Cartwright began one of the most hazardous attempts he had ever undertaken.

Carefully he climbed over to the seat in front, holding on grimly. He dropped beside Blackmore and put his lips to the detective's ear.

'I'm going to climb out on front,' he said. 'Slow her up for a second so that I can get a grip, and then let her out.'

The roadway was rushing past in a white blur, and Blackmore dare not take his eyes off the road even for a second. But he frowned and shook his head at Cartwright's daring suggestion.

'I'm going to try it!' said the secretary stubbornly. 'If Lumpert has to go under he'll see that the girl goes with him. We must try to get him before he can do any harm.'

It looked a suicidal plan, and even Turner was shouting to him not to do it. But Cartwright chose not to hear. He climbed out to the running board, bent low, and fought his way to the over-heated bonnet.

The detective eased the speed, for he knew that with the wind they were making, and the speed, the slightest jolt would be fatal. Cartwright never knew how he managed to keep the slender hold, but somehow he did it, and managed to straddle the bonnet and secure a firm grip on the metal work.

Lumpert had shot ahead when Blackmore eased down, and he had a clear lead of a quarter of a mile. In front of them was a level crossing. Lumpert cleared it, and to the detective's dismay, the gates began to move for a close. He pressed hard with his elbow on the klaxon. The shriek it made caused the man working the gates to stop, and in that second Blackmore sent the big car through, leaving but an inch between him and the gates.

It was only Blackmore's skill at the

wheel that kept them on the road. The tiniest error of judgment must have brought them unthinkable disaster, and Cartwright felt as if a thousand invisible hands were seeking to tear him from his flimsy hold.

But the detective was again closing on Lumpert, hand over hand. In two minutes he began to ease the speed, he was less than a hundred yards behind now, and still creeping in.

Now began the most difficult part of the job. He had to watch for any fractional lessening of the first car's pace so as to avoid a crash — he had to make sure that the other car was not able to shoot ahead again. Gradually he edged his car closer and closer until he was a scant six yards behind. Then the six yards were eaten up in as many seconds, and Cartwright's outstretched hand touched Lumpert's car!

Cramped and uncomfortable, buffeted by the wind their speed had aroused, Cartwright kept one thought grimly in his mind, the need for quick action once he touched the car.

Resting his hand on the polished panel of the car he got gingerly to his knees. Lumpert's car carried a luggage rack on it's roof and it afforded him a handgrip that made his attempt just possible.

John Blackmore did not pay any attention to Cartwright's action. He dared not. His job was to keep the car just behind the other, never allowing the few inches that remained between them to vary a hair's breadth. This he did, and sighed with relief when his secretary kicked clear and scrambled awkwardly on the roof of the other car.

Lumpert's car was still running steadily. Apparently he was not aware that he carried an extra passenger on the roof. Like Blackmore, he was forced to give all his attention to the road, more, he had to flash a glance now and then to the girl at his side.

Cartwright realised that a dangerous moment would come when his presence was revealed, for it was certain that Lumpert would refuse to pull up and tamely surrender. Creeping as silently as possible over the rack he peeped down and saw the professor, hatless, grimed with dirt, and with one half of his face masked by congealed blood from the wound.

Using the window frame for a foothold he swung round the angle and dropped on the footboard at Lumpert's side. The professor started as if he had been shot, then one hand lashed out at Cartwright's head. The secretary ducked and avoided the blow, but before he could climb in Lumpert's hand showed, and in it the steely blue of an automatic. It looked as if Cartwright must be killed.

And then unexpected help arrived. Mary Reed took a hand. Roused by the professor's lash at the young man's head, and seeing the pistol in his hand, she suddenly gripped the wrist that held it in both hands, and hung on gamely!

Lumpert tried to twist free, then jabbed his elbow into her ribs in a furious effort to fling her from him. The car was rocking wildly over the road, but she hung on until Cartwright was able to climb in and help her.

He tore Lumpert's hand from the

wheel, and kicked his foot from the accelerator. Mary Reed had edged right over to the door. Hanging on with one hand — the other was holding Lumpert's wrist — he began to ease the car from her dangerous rush. The speed was lessening every second now, and when he saw the bonnet of the grey car appear, and then shoot ahead of them, he thought that the danger was over.

But even he had not plumbed the depths of this maniac's mind. The sight of Blackmore's car told him that escape was impossible, and he stopped struggling and chuckled. The gun dropped from his fingers and the grip on the girl's wrist relaxed.

Then he played his last trick. Free of the girl's grip he swung his fist into Cartwright's face. As he fell backwards the professor pushed back the door catch and the secretary went sprawling into the road. He whirled the wheel half round stepped on the accelerator and sent the car straight at the one driven by the detective.

There was a rip of metal and the

double report of burst tyres. So terrific was the impact that the locked cars swerved and skidded in a quarter circle and then tore madly into the low stone wall that lined the road. The wheel was torn from Blackmore's hand, and he was thrown over the wall. Turner, too, was flung over. He landed heavily on the detective's shoulder and they rolled together until they were pulled up by a thick bush opposite.

The grey car had not escaped scot free, but her troubles were light when compared with those of the professor's car. There was a sickening smash. Somehow it had parted from the other car and had hit a telegraph pole. The pole stood, but the car collapsed.

Mary Reed felt as if a steam hammer had crashed into her back, as she took a neat header from the car to the roadside. As the stones rushed up to meet her she instinctively flung both hands forward. The skin peeled away, but the action saved her face and probably worse injuries.

But the strain of that over-crowded

minute had been too much, and she lay in the road in a faint. The next thing she remembered was Cartwright bending over her. As her eyes opened the anxious look on his face gave way to a smile.

'I'm so glad you're not dead,' he said. 'Keep still for a minute.'

Mary smiled wanly.

'What's happened to Dick, and Mr. Blackmore?' she asked fearfully.

'They're all right. They are full of bruises and plenty of skin missing, but nothing worse,' answered the young man.

'And — and that awful man?'

The smile left Cartwright's face.

'He got what he deserved,' he said. 'He hit the telegraph pole — head on.'

He said no more of Lumpert's terrible injuries, and the girl was wise enough not to ask questions. She could well imagine the result. She struggled to her feet and saw that Turner and the detective were bending over a heap in the road, covered by a rug, and waited until they turned away. They both looked white and sick, but on seeing the girl conscious they hurried to her side.

'Are you all right, Mary?' asked Turner anxiously. 'It's all over now. We are quite safe!'

'How do you feel, Miss Reed?' asked the detective.

'Not too bad,' said the girl. 'Are you sure you are both all right?'

They assured her that there were no bones broken, and that their trouble was only a few minor bruises.

'We can't stay here,' said the detective. 'There's still work to be done.'

The trio looked surprised, for with the end of Lumpert they had imagined that the affair was over.

'Barnes was in the car when the professor left Millhaven,' said the detective quietly. 'But he wasn't there when the crash came. I should think that when Lumpert slowly climbed over the first hill Barnes must have thrown himself out and hid in the rough ground. What men were left at the nursing home would not have been far away. And with him and Barton still free there is work ahead!'

17

Barton's Coup

About an hour after Professor Lumpert's sensational death on the Yorkshire Moors, the man posing as Jim Ayres strode purposefully into the office of the big spinning mill in Dipton.

The thirty clerks in the main office became exceedingly busy at the sight of the new master, for the few days he had spent in the place had already shown him a tyrant who exacted unquestioning obedience from those in his pay.

Beyond a curt nod for the chief clerk, he frowned at every glance turned his way. Hurrying to the comfortably furnished office, he flung hat and coat on the chair and began an uneasy pacing of the thick carpet.

'I'd give anything to know what happened at Millhaven,' he muttered to himself. 'Another twenty-four hours and we would have been through with the job. Nothing would have mattered then.' He paused opposite the window and stared down at the busy street below. 'Either the wireless has broken down or something very queer has overtaken Lumpert and Barnes. Can't understand it. Not a word from either of them, and the meeting due to start in an hour.'

His uneasy glance fell on a familiar blue-painted car slowly by the mill gate, and a look of relief swept over his face.

It was Lumpert's car, and it looked like Barnes at the wheel. He imagined that they had had a breakdown, and that his cause for worry was unfounded.

But when Jake Barnes came heavily into his office, the scowling face and manner showed that there was ample need to worry.

'So you haven't gone yet,' said Barnes, dropping wearily into the nearest chair. 'Thought you would have hopped off hours ago. You'd better go now, anyway.'

'What's the trouble, Jake?' asked Jim Barton. 'You know I must stick it for today. If all goes well I'll be out of Dipton for ever, an hour after the meeting.'

'If you're wise you'll be out in five minutes,' grunted Barnes. 'Or you'll be in prison one minute after Blackmore gets here.'

'Are you getting cold feet, Jake?' said Barton bitingly. 'Whatever Blackmore suspects he can't prove that I'm not Jim Ayres. Before he can, I'll have skipped it to where he'll never find me.'

Tired as he was Jake Barnes stared in amazement. After all he had gone through it seemed impossible that not a whisper had yet reached his partner in Dipton. He had no knowledge, of course, of the chase that Blackmore had been forced into — and it would have pleased him had he known that the chase had ended in one of the wildest parts of the moors. As it was he laughed harshly at his partner's ignorance, and quickly put him wise to the upsetting of all their carefully laid plans.

'Jim, you're a fool!' he said. 'You're standing on a volcano. If Blackmore doesn't know everything by now then I'll be damned! You just listen to what happened to me last night. Then tell me if you feel like sitting down in comfort.'

'All right,' sneered Barton. 'Get on with it. Have you got the wind up?'

But his face lengthened and fear lit up his eyes as he listened to Barnes' tale. Beginning with the surprise of Blackmore's appearance outside Millhaven at dawn, he told of the terrific explosion that had wrecked the old castle and of his own subsequent adventures.

'He handcuffed me and tied me up so that I couldn't stir an inch,' he said bitterly. 'He threw me into the car and left that damned girl to guard me. He and Turner beat it to the old house, and I hoped the place would fall down and bury them! They were away so long that I began to think my hopes had come true. Then all at once they came streaking out of the house, shouting as if the professor had fixed them. I didn't get the idea at first, but when Lumpert himself, all wounded and bleeding, suddenly jumped forward and grabbed the girl from under Blackmore's nose, I began to guess there was some fireworks about to play. And I wasn't wrong, Jim. Lumpert nearly pushed that car over the hill, and I nearly choked with shock.'

'Get on with the story, and not so much frillings,' snapped Barton impatiently.

'Lumpert was clever. He'd taken the girl and Blackmore just had to hop after him,' grinned Barnes. 'A bit of luck and he would have broken his neck. That grey racer of his plunged down the hill like it had taken wings — and by then Lumpert was crawling up again!'

'Well, how did it end?' asked Barton.

'Don't know! I didn't fancy a dash over England, tied up like I was,' said Barnes. 'I took a chance, pitched headlong out of the car, and lay quiet until they'd all beat it over the moors. Last I saw of them Lumpert had a mile lead, and they looked like going on for a week.'

'And what happened to you?'

'Why, Stern and the other fellows — what was left of them — came up from the cave entrance and untied me,' answered Jake Barnes. 'I didn't have much time to listen to them, but it appears that Blackmore got into the cave after that secretary of his, and drove Lumpert and the boys through to the sea. The professor apparently sent them a Mills bomb, blocked the way, and thought he had stopped Blackmore for ever. Well, he didn't, but five of our men have gone under, and Chee's out as well, so they said.

'And Jim Ayres? Was he buried in the ruins?'

'No!' said Barnes scowling, then his face cleared and he smiled wryly.

'As soon as I fired I asked about him. It appears he was with Seymour down in the cave, collecting the bits left over after the fight. I left Stern and the others going after them, and if they had got away we'd have heard about it by now.'

'Then it comes to this, Jake,' said Barton quickly. 'The game is up, as far as Millhaven is concerned. Lumpert and his nicotine gang are finished. That profitable game is blown sky high.'

'Maybe Lumpert is sky-high, seeing the speed he was going,' said Barnes.

'That doesn't matter, if he keeps

Blackmore busy for a few hours,' answered Barton brutally. 'He doesn't count. If we once get our hands on that pile he's got to find us — and we'll take some finding, Jake.'

Barnes stared.

'You're going through with it, after all?' he asked. 'After what I've told you? Why, Blackmore — '

'Blackmore be hanged!' said Barton viciously. 'If Lumpert hasn't done him in why haven't we heard from him before now?'

'Perhaps they've done each other in. Lumpert was madder than a stung snake, and they were doing quite seventy along that lumpy road,' said Barnes hopefully, never dreaming how near he was to the truth.

'It's us I'm worrying about,' said Barton. 'Stern has stopped Ayres from squealing, and maybe Blackmore and the others are in the mortuary by now. I want two clear hours — it's a big picking to run away from. And maybe it's only a shadow we're scared of.'

Barnes' eyes narrowed, and he was

thoughtfully silent for a full minute. Then he suddenly jumped to his feet and grasped Barton's hand.

'I'm sticking to you, Jim,' he exclaimed. 'We'll never have a pile of money dangling in front of us like this again. That is — if the fools bite quick.'

Barton laughed over the doubt.

'I've played them very well,' he said. 'When they come in here you'll see three sturdy Englishmen ripe for the plucking. You had better go and get cleaned up. Remember, you're my pal, over there, and I'm the blue-eyed innocent who wants to get out from a game I'm scared of. You understand, Jake?'

'I do!' said Barnes briefly. 'Where do I get this wash?'

Just thirty minutes later the three 'sturdy Englishmen' were ushered into the private office — three prominent members of the Lancashire cotton industry, who had been invited to the greatest bargain sale on record.

The quietly spoken young man who asked them to be seated at the table was Jim Ayres, so far as they were concerned,

274

owner of this busy mill that employed nearly three thousand hands.

'Gentlemen, we'll get right down to business,' he said with a frank smile. 'To be truthful, I'm a little scared of you Englishmen. It seems to me that the cotton industry is a fighting game of dog-eat-dog, and I'm the bone with the meaty pickings.'

The chairman of the Spinners' Federation laughed.

'I don't think we are quite as bad as that, Mr. Ayres,' he said. 'But the business is strange to you, and I understand you've decided to get out of it?'

'You're quite right, Mr. Johnson,' agreed Barton.

'Well, you've sent us certified copies of your accounts, and I must say they make good reading,' Johnson replied. 'You wish to make a quick sale to get back to America?'

'I would like to go back on to-morrow's boat from Liverpool,' said Barton. 'And as it is a rush job I'm willing to sell out cheap.'

'You see, Jim is my partner in a

Mexican Silver mine,' Barnes chimed in. 'We've big interests there. If he doesn't come back quickly I'm afraid somebody will be doing us out of our profits.'

'Quite,' assented Johnson. 'We have considered the figures, Mr. Ayres, and we are willing to offer you two hundred and fifty thousand pounds, for the plant and goodwill of the Ayres Spinning Mill.' He held up his hand before Barton could speak. 'That is, if our accountant is satisfied with certain questions he wishes to ask you.'

'I told you this was to be a private meeting,' said Barton frowning. 'I've no time to answer questions — it is to be a quick sale or nothing. If you don't want the business I've other people after it. I'm due to see a man this afternoon.'

'But we do want it,' said Johnson quickly. 'We won't waste any of your time, for we've brought Mr. Blackmore along with us now.'

'Mister — who?' shouted Barton, jumping to his feet in alarm.

The Lancashire mill-owners looked surprised at this outburst.

'Mr. Blackmore — Mr. Robert Blackmore, our accountant,' explained Johnson mildly. 'He wants you to satisfy him on one or two little points, then the business is through.'

'Well, let him come in,' said Barton briefly. He glanced meaningly at Barnes and nodded to the door. 'Jake, you go and get this Robert Blackmore — we'll hear what he has to say, eh?'

Barnes scowled and made for the door. He reappeared in about ten seconds, but the scowl had gone from his face by then. In fact he smiled and nodded brightly to Barton.

'Mr. Robert Blackmore, Jim,' he announced. 'He's all right, I don't think he will annoy you.'

The man who now advanced nervously to the table certainly looked incapable of annoying anybody. He was old and bent, with thin white hair flattened untidily over his forehead, and he wore big, steel rimmed spectacles, through which his eyes twinkled. A walrus moustache of iron grey hid his mouth, he looked about as helpless and harmless a being as Barton had seen for a long time.

'Come in, Mr. Blackmore,' said Barton cheerfully. 'You've got something to say about this sale, I think?'

'A very generous offer you've made,' said the man. He sat in a chair at the bottom of the long table and took a bundle of papers from a leather case. 'Ah, the Ayres mill made a profit of nearly forty thousand pounds last year, sir?'

'The accounts tell you so,' snapped Barton.

'Oh, quite! quite!' said the old chap hastily. 'Yet you only want a quarter of a million for the whole business?'

'Yes, but I want a lot of it in cash,' said Barton quickly.

'That's just it. It's so unusual, sir,' Robert Blackmore said apologetically. 'You ask for fifty thousand in cash. Most irregular, sir.'

'Is that so?' sneered Barton nastily. 'I'd look nice if I was out of England with your cheque and found I'd been sold a pup!' His first crashed down on the table. 'No, sir! I'm scared of you smooth tongue cotton kings, and I mean to see the colour of your money before I give up this valuable property!'

'You want to take an awful lot of money away with you, sir,' the old man said, adding nervously, 'There are such a lot of undesirable people about, you might lose it,'

'Not very likely!' Barton laughed harshly.

He turned contemptuously from the old man to Johnson.

'If you've got the money and want the property say so. If you don't — good-day!'

'Really, Robert, I think we had better humour him,' Mr. Johnson smiled. He took a cheque book from his pocket, picked up a pen and began to fill in the amount. 'If you'll take this cheque to the Westminster — '

'Mr. Johnson, please,' said the old man sharply. 'I do want to impress on Mr. Ayres what he is doing.'

'Impress nothing!' said Barton.

'But I must!' insisted Robert Blackmore. 'I have been learning things this morning. I must ask you to listen to me!'

He still kept his mild air, but now the weak old man seemed to have become the centre of attraction. He took a slip of paper from his case, settled the glasses more firmly on his nose, and glanced nervously at the mill-owner.

'On Monday you drew seven thousand pounds from your bank — in cash, sir,' he began. 'The next day it was twelve thousand — in cash. To-day it was again seven — and again in cash!'

'Well, why not? It's mine isn't it?' drawled Barton. 'I'll have that bank manager fired for giving my affairs publicity! But what has it got to do with you?'

Quite suddenly the air had become electric.

'Only this, sir,' the old fellow said quietly. 'With Mr. Johnson's cheque cashed you'll be leaving the country with seventy-five thousand pounds in cash!'

'And why not. I said, it's mine, isn't it?' Barton again demanded.

'That's just what I'm wondering,' Robert answered slowly.

'What do you mean, you old fool?'

Barnes suddenly chipped in. 'Jim owns the mill — '

'But this fellow doesn't!'

The old man's nervous manner had vanished, and he rapped out the words. Even as he spoke he swept wig, glasses and whiskers from his face with one move, snatched a gun from his pocket, and sat with it pointed at Barton.

'John Blackmore!' The words were a whisper, but they reached the detective. He glared round at the three mill-owners venomously. 'Trying to double-cross me on an honest deal — '

'Shut up, Barton!' snapped the detective. 'And put your hands on the table. You too, Barnes. I'm taking no chances with you!'

'But what does it all mean?' said Mr. Johnson weakly, flinching away from the pointed gun. 'You're not the accountant from Messrs. Crealy — though you look like him. Who are you, sir?'

'John Blackmore,' said the detective, tersely. 'And I've been watching these crooks for days. Are you coming quietly, you two? Lumpert is dead, and your game is stone cold now.'

'All right, spy!' said Barton. 'You've got us, and we're coming quietly — when you get us!'

He spat the last four words at the detective, and as he uttered them Barton brought his knees sharply up under the table. The light wood tilted, and Barnes instantly ducked and sent it crashing over on Blackmore's head!

It was a quick trick, and one that had served these American toughs in many a wild fight. Blackmore leaped aside with but a second to spare, but the terrified Johnson barged heavily into him, and they dropped to the floor together.

18

The 'Bishop' at Bay

It was the unluckiest accident imaginable, for while Blackmore was still pinned down by Johnson, the two crooks jumped for a door behind them. In the opening Barton turned and fired a shot at the fallen detective. It stung an inch past his ear and started a panic in the outer office.

'Get out of the way!' shouted the detective to the man on top of him. 'If those men get loose God knows what damage they will do!'

He was through the door and into the mill in a flash, but luck was against him. The frenzied dash of the crooks had caused an uproar in the place, and Barton had cleverly traded on the fact that he was Jim Ayres and the 'boss.'

'There's a madman after us,' he shouted, speeding through the packed room. 'Make way for him!'

Blackmore's appearance with a gun in his hand was the signal for a wild rush to the exit, with the result that they were hopelessly blocked a second after the Americans had gone through.

Girls were screaming, and men were shouting to each other. A few of the more plucky ones bore down on Blackmore, grabbing spanners and anything they could lay hands on.

'That man is not Jim Ayres!' shouted the detective. 'He's a crook, and you're helping them to get away! Let me through!'

'It's Blackmore!' shouted a voice. 'I saw him at the inquest. 'Come on, sir. Get out of the way!'

By now Barton and Barnes had raced through the time-keeper's office and out into a side street. Turning for the front of the building where Barnes' car stood, they were within twenty feet of it when a second car came speeding down the street, and drew up with grinding brakes.

Cartwright, with Inspector Moore, and two other men scrambled out on to the pavement. A van crowded with uniformed men stopped in front of Barnes's car, and the two crooks realised that their dash for freedom had been made a second too late.

Mad with rage, Barton fired two shots, and Moore spun dizzily round and clutched the side of the car.

'They've got me in the shoulder!' he said. 'After them, they're making for the mill!'

Knowing the penalty of capture, the two men had become utterly indifferent as to what damage they might do. Jumping the steps to the main office Barton cruelly clubbed one man who tried to stop him, and Barnes fired point-blank at another. Blackmore arrived on the spot three seconds after they had gone into the mill again, and he lost no time in explanations.

'Put men at all exits!' he shouted to the sergeant-in-charge. 'Get the people out of the place! I'll keep them busy until you've surrounded the mill!'

He guessed that Barton was hoping to find a quiet exit that would give him a chance of getting away unseen. In a huge building like a mill there are a hundred windows and often a dozen doors to get out of. With the confusion that reigned the crooks might easily get lost in the crowd, and the detective meant to prevent that at all costs.

But he was not alone in that idea. Cartwright stuck to his side, and Ayres and Seymour were not far behind — they had suffered enough already to make the hunting of the crooks a matter of cold business.

An outburst of screams told the detective in which way the two men were making, and he smiled grimly as the meaning of the the shouts came to him. Barton had started the report that an armed madman was loose in the building, and the rumour had spread like wildfire. Now the sight of the two armed and raging men was the signal for a fresh panic. They were mistaken for the madman, and every door and window was thronged with people trying to get out.

'They've gone upstairs!' shouted Cartwright. 'If there's a fire escape — '

'Bound to be!' said the detective, 'and that's their last hope, and they know it!'

They caught sight of the two men on the second floor. Crouched down behind the railings at the top of the stairs they opened fire on Blackmore and his little company, shots that went wide because the fellows were shaken and trembling in their desperate effort to get away.

A bullet went through Cartwright's sleeve, and the secretary shouted as the hot metal ripped the skin. Blackmore's answer was swift and exacting. He fired once. Barnes' gun kicked from his hand, he screamed with pain, and started nursing a shattered wrist.

Then the real Jim Ayres let go with a weapon he had picked up in the cave. His first bullet sang dangerously close to Barton's head, the second hit the railing by his face, and an iron chip made a crimson streak across the fellow's fore-head. That was enough. The pair fled again, and there was only the roof left for them now.

At the end of the top floor machine room Barton discovered a cubby hole, but more important to them was an iron ladder that showed the way to a trap-door.

Blackmore, Cartwright, Ayres, Seymour and some of the workmen were soon after them. Blackmore mounted the ladder cautiously and ventured a peep over the coping. He expected a bullet to come winging his way, and was ready to dodge out of sight at first sight of the gun-men. But the place was deserted and silent, there was no sign or sound of the two men he was hunting.

Climbing out on to the roof he realised at once that taking these men was going to be a dangerous job. Huge angled skylights filled the middle of the roof, with several chimney stacks at regular intervals.

For a moment Blackmore hesitated to expose his companions to the danger of such an ambush. Barton and Barnes must be hiding behind one of these stacks, and they could fire and retreat until surrounded. Glancing down he could see that the street below was packed with an excited throng, and he was wondering if it would be better to try and starve the men out when the matter was settled for him.

Cartwright climbed out to the roof, followed by Ayres and Seymour, both armed and ready for trouble.

'The devils can give some trouble before we get them,' said the secretary as he took in the position.

'They'll never let us take them,' said the detective. 'They must know by now that this is the end, and the police will have no mercy.'

'Don't let's wait for the police,' said Ayres. 'I don't know who this fellow is, but he's not getting away with what he did to the old man.'

'I'll tell you who he is — ' began the detective, but Jim Ayres was already creeping round the off-side of the sky-light and in a second was out of sight.

'That settles it,' said Blackmore. 'Barton will kill him if we leave them to fight it out alone.'

Seymour followed Ayres, meaning to be in at the finish. Blackmore and Cartwright crept along the knee high coping, bending low, and never taking their eyes off the first chimney stack.

Ten feet away from them they suddenly

saw Barton's face pop up between the pots, and a bullet zipped the framework a few inches from the detective's hand. It was a good shot for a sudden snap, but Blackmore's answering bullet must have caught the man, for there was a scurrying of feet on the leads that told them the men were not yet cornered.

Running towards the stack Blackmore and his secretary were in time to see an amazing sight. Barnes, with shattered wrist, had lagged a little behind his more active leader, and as Blackmore called to them to give in he slipped and fell half over the coping. With two sound hands Barnes could have eased himself over. With one smashed he clawed weakly at the stone, and began to slip backwards. He was half sitting, half lying over a hundred foot drop.

Suddenly from the other side came a shout.

'Barton! Drop that gun! Get out here and we'll finish the fight we started in Alaska!'

It was Jim Ayres, he had worked his way round to the rear of Barton, and for the first time saw the face of the man he was hunting.

Barton lifted his automatic, pressed the trigger, but nothing happened. His hand went to his hip, but before he had time to make use of the gun that was always there Seymour fired.

For a second Barton stood, his hand pressed to his chest, swaying, and then, before anyone could reach him he fell. His shoulder hit the low coping and to their horror he pitched headlong down, into the street below.

As soon as Blackmore noticed the silence of Barton's gun he had run to the help of Barnes. The man was hauled to safety, but there was another wound in his shoulder, near the neck. The detective laid him down and was in time to see the 'Bishop' fall to his death.

★ ★ ★

Three hours later the town of Dipton had settled to something like ordinary behaviour again. The mill had closed down for the day following the affairs earlier. The town was buzzing with rumours concerning the fight on the roof. Everybody had their own tale, but nobody but the group in the sitting-room of the Dipton Hotel really knew the truth.

'I can't understand how you came to be on the scene so quickly,' said Blackmore to his secretary. 'I left you on the moors with Turner and Miss Reed, with orders to go back to Lumpert's house and see how Ayres and Seymour were getting on.'

Cartwright smiled, and winked across at Jim Ayres.

'Well, I did,' he said, 'and found them resting comfortably downstairs. If I had known we were coming back here to have lumps shot off us we would have stayed away.'

Mary Reed turned to Dick Turner with a smile.

'I think you had better tell Mr. Blackmore what happened,' she said.

'Well, plenty happened,' said Turner. 'Lumpert's men had these two penned in a cave; they weren't bothering about their own wounded. Cartwright borrowed some policemen from the village on the way back. He went ahead with the bobbies and had the professor's men on the run by the time we got there. We caught five of Lumpert's men, and they are waiting in the local police station until you charge them.'

'And the moment Cartwright got us out of the cave he must needs start chasing back to Dipton,' said Ayres. 'Said he couldn't leave you on your own. I thought he was your secretary, not a nurse,' he smiled.

The detective's eyes twinkled.

'He often gets that way,' he said.

'But, Mr. Blackmore,' said his secretary. 'You haven't told us the half of things yet. Millhaven was a crook's nest, and it wasn't opened for the sake of kidnapping Mr. Ayres, you know all the answers, why not let us in on the secret?'

'Lumpert was a professional poisoner,' said Blackmore, 'open for hire by any crook who could pay his fee. Take the case of Seymour, and he was only one of several. Seymour is very wealthy, and a distant cousin wanted his money. So Seymour disappeared, and Lumpert has been blackmailing the cousin ever since.'

'Seymour will be out of hospital in a month's time. I shouldn't like to be his cousin then!' said Ayres. 'But what about me, Mr. Blackmore? How does my old enemy, the 'Bishop' come into the Dipton Mill affair?'

Blackmore hesitated.

'You'll have to know some time, Ayres,' he said slowly. 'So I might as well tell you now. Jim Barton was your half-brother. You were both the sons of old Jacob Ayres!'

'Good Heavens!' gasped Jim Ayres. 'And we hunted each other up and down Alaska for months with guns in our hands!'

'And ended the fight on your own roof,' said the detective.

He told Ayres of the letters found in the weaving shed, and explained what had happened since Morris received them.

'You can imagine Morris' bitter hatred of Ayres when he returned from America, and his longing to find his sister's child. It's easy enough to guess that when he found Ayres making a fortune the idea came to him to use the old man's money to search for the child. It was years before he did find him, and then the fellow was in Sing-Sing working out a life sentence. It was then that Morris got into touch with Professor Lumpert.'

'You mean that Barton's escape from Sing-Sing was engineered from this town by Morris?' asked Cartwright.

Blackmore nodded.

'I am convinced that the warder who died the night Barton made his break was the victim of Lumpert's nicotine,' he answered. 'Barton was smuggled here, and then Morris' real troubles began. It was about that time that Morris started stealing huge sums from the mill. Barton was a complete waster. His extravagances nearly drove the old man crazy. And then when Morris was in a dreadful mess at the mill, came the news that the real Jim Ayres was on his way home. Morris must have passed on the news to Barton, and from that came the plot to kidnap you, Jim, and kill your father. You were tricked into leaving the ship, and one of Lumpert's men actually had the cheek to take your place when a Scotland Yard man came to tell you of the sudden death of your father.'

'But why was Morris killed in the grounds of my father's house if he was in the plot with Barton?' asked Jim Ayres.

'We found that out in London,' said the detective. 'The night we went to Chee Fu's place and overhead the conversation between Chee and Barnes we found out the reason. Morris thought the concoction Lumpert had given him would only make the mill-owner unfit to look after the business. When he found that it would kill him, and that he was on his way to becoming a murderer, he rushed back to Dipton, but word of his return had been sent on by Chee and he never had a chance of warning Jacob Ayres.'

'But why didn't they kill me, and Barton keep my identity and money?' asked Ayres.

'He was only moderately like you, that's why,' said the detective. 'The first person who had known you in America would have seen the fraud at once. He just wanted to impersonate you for one week, in order to clear off with something like a hundred thousand pounds. He nearly succeeded.'

'I know,' said Ayres, 'and if it hadn't been for you and Cartwright he would have done it.'

'They were trying to keep suspicion away from the house for the few days they needed,' said the detective. 'Morris was killed outside the study, Barton was inside posing as you. They didn't want the police looking round. They had to get rid of the body, and Morris was known to have quarrelled with Dick Turner, so they did their best to lay the blame of the killing on you, Turner.'

'And Moore was willing to give me all the blame that was knocking round,' said Dick.

John Blackmore lit a cigarette.

'We're returning to London on the night train,' he said. 'So if there are any more questions you'd like to ask — '

'There is one,' said Ayres. 'The question of your fee, and Cartwright's. You've saved my life, and my bank balance, and I'm hanged if I know what to do about it.'

There was a short pause, and the detective looked at his secretary.

'You dragged me into this,' he said, 'so — you'll name the fee.'

'That's easy,' said Cartwright, with a broad grin. 'Mr. Ayres, you've got a lot of people working for you, suppose you build them a good club-house — and make Mr. Blackmore come down and give the opening speech?'

'I'm willing,' said Ayres.

And Cartwright laughed, for he knew that if there was one thing in the world Blackmore was afraid of it was making speeches.